"Orgasms are bi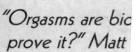
prove it?" Matt

Bridget laughed. And it made him smile.

"Exactly what hypothesis would you offer to prove?"

He took her into his arms. "The main physical changes that occur during a sexual experience are a result of vasocongestion."

"English, please." She stepped back.

"It means accumulation of blood in various parts of the body. Muscular tension increases and other——"

"Correct me if I'm wrong, but in an experiment, doesn't the scientist perform?"

Matt grinned and pulled her close again. "As a scientist who's very interested in experimenting on you, I can say I definitely can perform."

"Talk, talk, talk. How about some action?" And she twined her arms around his neck.

He hesitated, recognizing the danger, but decided for once in his life he wasn't going to plan things out. The bottom line was he wanted her. He wanted her badly. And he would now stop at nothing to have her.

Blaze™

Dear Reader,

People go to a lot of trouble to find themselves. Some walk a spiritual path, others go on the trip of their dreams and some find that what they were so desperately searching for is right in their own backyard.

Bridget Cole can relate. She returns to Cambridge, Massachusetts, after losing key modeling contracts in New York City. But she's convinced that she'll return to the Big Apple to regain what she's lost. She doesn't bank on sexy Matt Fox, her childhood friend and the boy next door. At sixteen, she dared him to kiss her in an intimate game of truth or dare and she has never gotten over it. Now Matt's back on the scene and looking to pick up where they left off....

I thank you for taking the time to read my book and hope it brings you much enjoyment. Let me know. Drop me a line in care of Harlequin Books, 225 Duncan Mill Road, Don Mills, Ontario M3B 3K9, Canada, or visit my Web site at www.karenanders.com.

Happy reading!

Karen Anders

Books by Karen Anders

HARLEQUIN BLAZE

*Women Who Dare

KAREN ANDERS
Almost Naked, Inc.

HARLEQUIN®

TORONTO • NEW YORK • LONDON
AMSTERDAM • PARIS • SYDNEY • HAMBURG
STOCKHOLM • ATHENS • TOKYO • MILAN • MADRID
PRAGUE • WARSAW • BUDAPEST • AUCKLAND

If you purchased this book without a cover you should be aware that this book is stolen property. It was reported as "unsold and destroyed" to the publisher, and neither the author nor the publisher has received any payment for this "stripped book."

To Melanie Martin for her friendship and pink pop-ups.
A special thanks to Marlies Durso for her invaluable help
with all things relating to the fashion industry
and to Liz Quigley for her insights on the inner
workings of the garden club.
All mistakes are mine.

ISBN 0-373-79197-6

ALMOST NAKED, INC.

Copyright © 2005 by Karen Alarie.

All rights reserved. Except for use in any review, the reproduction or utilization of this work in whole or in part in any form by any electronic, mechanical or other means, now known or hereafter invented, including xerography, photocopying and recording, or in any information storage or retrieval system, is forbidden without the written permission of the publisher, Harlequin Enterprises Limited, 225 Duncan Mill Road, Don Mills, Ontario, Canada M3B 3K9.

All characters in this book have no existence outside the imagination of the author and have no relation whatsoever to anyone bearing the same name or names. They are not even distantly inspired by any individual known or unknown to the author, and all incidents are pure invention.

This edition published by arrangement with Harlequin Books S.A.

® and TM are trademarks of the publisher. Trademarks indicated with ® are registered in the United States Patent and Trademark Office, the Canadian Trade Marks Office and in other countries.

www.eHarlequin.com

Printed in U.S.A.

Prologue

Truth or Dare—Twelve years ago

BRIDGET COLE'S FACE was classically beautiful, and even from a distance her skin looked creamy and flawless. Her hair tumbled down her back to her waist, the color of opulent amber—a budding woman who was all pink cotton candy seduction and mouth-watering honey.

The focus of Matthew Fox's fantasies stood at the bottom of the basement stairs talking to a dark-haired girl.

He noticed every shift her body made as she smiled and nodded her head at something the other girl said.

The short striped pink miniskirt left her smooth, slender thighs bare and fueled his imagination and male hormones. He knew it was one of her designs. She'd showed him the sketch of the skirt last week, saying softly that her mother thought it was just doo-dling. Deft with a needle and thread, she'd made the pink concoction from her own pattern.

But it wasn't the clothing that interested him as he

took in the view, his gaze sliding upward. His mouth went dry as he took in curvaceous hips, a slim waist and a top that molded to ample, perfectly rounded breasts and showed the faint outline of her nipples pressing against the pink, stretchy fabric of her top.

At sixteen, he was now quite well aware of what it meant to want someone in the physical sense, except he had all these pent-up feelings for her that were quite inconvenient. Hormones won out, a hard thing to swallow as Matt prided himself on his intellect. He cut himself a break, since he was, after all, a teenage boy.

She had soft, full lips and a sweet mouth designed to give all kinds of erotic pleasure. The thought caused his stomach to tighten with awareness and made other parts of his anatomy leap to attention, as well.

He caught her eye and she smiled like an angel. Matt felt everything inside him tense. A jumble of feelings and emotions only made him all the more confused, caught between his body's needs and his mind's awareness.

Bridget was a complication Matt didn't know how to handle.

Bridget was his friend.

A very beautiful and sexy friend who had grown from a petite blond dynamo to a sleek, sophisticated sixteen-year-old girl.

They were worlds apart. She was on the beauty pageant circuit and he was headed for a prestigious college. Her parents were wealthy. His parents weren't. He liked math and she hated it. A girl that was so far out of his league, he was crazy to even think he had a chance with her.

Her party was in full swing and they were all in the basement to play Trivial Pursuit. With her no-holds-barred attitude, Bridget had convinced her aunt to host this teen party without her mother's knowledge. He couldn't blame her aunt. He was also under Bridget's spell.

Bridget had personally invited him. Since he lived next door, he was a frequent visitor whenever Bridget visited her aunt. He also tutored Bridget in math and let her look through his telescope.

He stood off to the side, his back to the wall, his hands buried deep in his pockets.

Her other guests started to gather in a circle. Bridget started across the room and he couldn't take his eyes off her. The way she moved was a sensual feast. She stopped in front of him. "Let's play."

"Trivial Pursuit," he said, getting lost in her big blue eyes.

"Truth or Dare. It'll be much more fun."

As effectively as if she'd thrown cold water on him, he shut down. Shaking his head, he said, "No. Not interested."

"Come on, Bridget, leave the nerd alone. He doesn't want to play," said a spiky-haired blond guy who looked as if he could crush bricks in his hands.

"Shut up, Mike, and mind your own business," Bridget said, turning to the boy with a fierce look on her face. When she turned back around, she said softly. "Don't mind him. He can be a jerk."

Matt suspected the guy was a jerk, but he could care less what the jerk thought of him. He shrugged.

"Matt, you don't have to watch from the sidelines."

"I'm not playing, Bridget."

"Fine," she said, her blue eyes snapping. "Suit yourself."

Keeping his own counsel, he watched with a deep interest.

"Bridget, since it's your party, why don't you pick the person who'll go first?" the dark-haired girl said.

Bridget nodded and smiled easily. "How about you, Stephanie?"

"Okay," Stephanie said, singling out a curly redhead. "Tonia. Truth or dare."

The girl thought for a moment and said, "Dare."

Stephanie said, "The two closest members of the opposite sex get to slap your butt as hard as they want to! Bend over and take it with a smile!"

Tonia giggled and looked at the two boys next to her. Turning around, she presented her backside to them and each slapped her bottom. One boy harder than the other.

The redhead turned back around and said, "Brittany, truth or dare?"

The petite, blonde smiled shyly and said, "Truth."

"What was the most passionate moment you have ever experienced? Describe it for the group."

As the girl started talking, Matt watched Bridget who kept giving him surreptitious, frowning looks. As the game progressed, inevitably someone called out Bridget's name and she, of course, said, "Dare."

The person who called her name, a guy that Matt knew was friends with Mike said, "French-kiss Mike, locking tongues for fifteen seconds."

Matt tensed, his back pulling away from the wall, his hands tightening into fists deep in his pockets.

"Hey, it's time for party snacks," her aunt yelled from the top of the stairs, a few seconds warning before she started down. Bridget looked over her shoulder, gauging the time it would take her aunt to make it to the bottom. She turned back to the boy then looked up at Matt. Their eyes met and clung. Bridget's eyes widened as she stared at him. He was sure the fierce need to do bodily harm to a guy twice his size was clear in his eyes.

For the first time in his life, his withdrawal mechanism failed him. His innermost desires were visible in his eyes and Bridget finally knew how he felt about her. What he didn't know was how *she* felt about it.

Her smile faded. She pulled away from the boy's advance and sat back on her heels.

Her aunt appeared and began to usher everyone up the stairs. "Bridget?" she said, looking at her niece.

"I'll be up in a minute, Aunt Ida."

Her aunt took one look at Matt and nodded. She followed behind the retreating teens.

Bridget rose in that graceful, sexy way she moved and walked toward him. Stopping in front of him, she looked deep into his eyes. "Truth or dare, Matt?"

Caught off guard, he simply stared at her.

She stepped closer and her voice dropped an octave. "Truth or dare?"

He didn't know what made him say it. It came out of his mouth in a hoarse whisper. "Dare."

Blue fire danced in the depths of her eyes. "Kiss me."

Matt swallowed hard, caught up and held in that blue flame until it engulfed him completely. Lifting his hand, he touched the side of her throat. Her skin felt like rich warm velvet. She licked her lips and he honed in on them, dipping his head, moving slowly to savor each second, breathe in her scent, absorb the heat of her skin, anticipating the taste of her mouth.

"Matt," she breathed softly, the blue flames in her eyes burning hotter, kissing him with intense heat.

The feel of her lips beneath his was exquisite, warm and heated and undeniably demanding. When their tongues touched, then tangled silkily, fire licked through him, deep and low. She tasted forbidden and decadent, like wild, untamed lust, and he felt an amazing sense of himself as a boy on the brink of manhood.

He groaned at the incredible surge of hot, carnal lust that kicked up his adrenaline a few notches. He felt primal and possessive and ravenous; unable to get enough of this girl who affected him not only sexually, but on a deeper level he'd yet to fully define. All he knew was he had to have her, all her sass, her devil-may-care attitude, and her curvy, enticing body.

"Bridget!" her mother called from the top of the stairs and Bridget jumped away from Matt.

"Oh dammit. She *never* lets up," she cried, giving Matt an apologetic look before she headed for the stairs.

Too late. Her mother materialized at the bottom. She took one look at Matt and Bridget. Her mouth thinned as she shot daggers at him with those scary eyes.

She grabbed Bridget by the arm and dragged her up the stairs. He could hear her mother railing at Bridget for going behind her back and having a party.

Matt stood in the basement getting the terrible feeling he was never going to see her again. Dread formed a lead ball in his stomach as he leaned against the wall and closed his eyes.

There was something to be said for looking but not touching.

Now that he knew what it was like to touch her, he would never be the same again.

1

Twelve years later

ANTICIPATION THRUMMED like a taut wire through Matt's system as he turned at the sound of a car stopping at the curb. Like a sleek black panther, a stretch limo idled in front of the majestic twin columns of the Meadow Hills Country Club. He immediately thought that perhaps there were going to be celebrities at the fiftieth birthday bash Bridget Cole was throwing for her aunt Ida.

But when Bridget Cole's aunt emerged from the limo, the anticipation simmering inside him ever since Aunt Ida had invited him to the party, tightened into a hard ball in his gut.

Bridget's aunt wore a beautiful black gown with shiny beads that caught and reflected the light. Her blond hair was piled on top of her head in an elaborate upsweep that was very flattering for a woman who was turning fifty. But Bridget had a handsome family, her aunt included. He suspected good genes accounted for that.

Other people emerged from the limo: Bridget's

mother, who narrowed her eyes at him as if she couldn't quite place him, then her father and other people who he suspected were members of the family he hadn't met. They all paused next to the limo waiting for what looked like the last passenger. An enormous package tied with a gold ribbon appeared in the doorway of the limo clasped in delicate hands tipped with silver nails.

Out of the corner of his eye, he saw Bridget's mother touch her sister's arm and lean toward her to speak, but his attention was focused on the passenger behind the large gift.

Since no one stepped forward to help with the huge package, he approached the limo and took the beautifully wrapped gift that blocked his view of the seat beyond and the owner of those delicate hands.

His anticipation kicked up another agonized notch. One of the family members said thanks and took the present out of his hands. With a jolt, he came face-to-face with Bridget.

Matt heard Bridget suck in a quick breath and watched her eyes widen. Unbridled excitement hummed in the air as their eyes locked and held across the short space that separated them. For a moment they stared at each other, twelve years and a daring kiss separating them. "Matt," she said softly, a wealth of meaning embedded in his name.

The memory of her hot mouth, her loss of control, the soft way she melted into him came back to him tenfold even though it had happened when he was sixteen. Clearly it had been her first thought, too, a memory so tantalizing it was mirrored in her deep blue eyes—thickly lashed eyes that ensnared him and always seemed to have a dare in them.

"Are you going to help me out?"

"Sorry," he said stupidly and offered his open palm to her. She reached out and closed her fingers around his outstretched hand, the pads of her fingers nestling against his palm. The shock of her skin meeting his sent his mind into a tailspin.

She smiled. "Matt, you need to back up."

"Right," he said, taking a step back so that Bridget could fully exit the limo.

Dressed in a silver gown, she was stunning—as if light was absorbed into her and reflected back out with a dazzling luminosity. The bodice molded to her breasts like a second skin, the straps crossing her collarbone to tie around the neck, leaving her back bare. Although he'd seen her glossy photo in too many magazines to name, dressed in many different ways, including racy ads in almost nothing but her skin, the sheer magnitude of her presence overwhelmed him. Seeing Bridget in the flesh again opened all the floodgates of tangled-up emotion and desire. Matt could only stand there with a sinking heart, realizing that Bridget had moved even further out of his reach.

Now, more than time separated them.

BRIDGET SAT at the head table eating with her aunt and the rest of her family, but she couldn't stop searching the room for Matt's face.

The last time she'd seen him before tonight, he'd been standing against her aunt Ida's basement wall, looking tortured and hot as sin. The short, skinny adolescent with the shock of dark hair and exotic eyes had changed into a tall, leanly muscled teenager, his dark hair tousled around his head, his devastating brown eyes glittering with potent male heat as he offered up a silent challenge to her. Mike had called him a nerd out of stupid male rivalry, but at sixteen, Matt was anything but. She'd been blindsided by her own emotions that afternoon, the deep-seated friendship morphing into something more dangerous, more intoxicating and wholly forbidden.

The kiss they had shared had been the steamiest in her sixteen years and even in her naiveté, she had wanted something more from him. But she'd never gotten the chance to find out. Her mother had been so furious that night she had forbidden Bridget to visit her aunt. Her mother upped the pageant show entries and Bridget had been so busy traveling and winning that she'd never gotten the chance to see Matt again. It hurt her feelings that he hadn't ever tried to get in touch with her.

Ever since she could remember, Matt had lived next door to her favorite aunt. He'd always tried to cheer her up when her mother made her cry. He had been her sounding board, her conscience and her friend. That was until that kiss in the basement of her aunt's house.

While Bridget was chasing fame and fortune, Matt had changed—a lot. He still had those deep fathomless eyes, slightly tipped at the corners. Eyes that seemed to hold the wealth of the universe in them, but his face had matured into a man's. A gorgeous man at that. His shoulders had widened and his chest broadened. He still had that smart, studious air about him, a calm, detached demeanor that made her want to rile him up and see what happened.

Something shifted inside her, a tightness settling around her heart. It wouldn't matter how she felt about Matt right now or ever. Their paths had diverged completely. Bridget wanted what modeling could bring her—the fast life. Matt, on the other hand, was very much settled into the academic life, a slow life that was far removed from her world of glamour and parties.

But seeing Matt now and remembering that breath-stealing kiss sent her hormones into an overwhelming frenzy of sexual longing. Her breasts swelled and tightened, her nipples tingled. She couldn't help thinking that maybe, while she was in Cambridge, she could settle her curiosity and have her wicked way with him. There was something to be said for going slow.

She'd had her share of lovers during her modeling career, but they couldn't wipe out the memory of that kiss. She was suddenly wondering what it would feel like if she were skin-to-skin close to Matt.

"Aunt Ida," Bridget said, leaning closer to her aunt. "I didn't know Matt was in Cambridge."

"He just moved back."

"I thought you said something about him working in North Carolina."

"He was. You'll have to ask him the particulars. He's a sweet boy. He cuts my grass for me. You two haven't been back in the same neighborhood for a long time. I'm sure you have a lot of catching up to do."

"Yes, we do." Bridget searched the crowd again for Matt.

"I'm sorry we couldn't make it to Australia this year, honey. The hospital needs me."

"I'm disappointed, but I understand being a nurse is very important to you, Aunt Ida. We've been to some wonderful places."

"Yes, but Australia can wait until next year. It'll give me a full year to plan. Thank you for throwing this lavish party. You know you didn't have to."

"I know that, but I wanted to. I'll throw one for Mom when she turns fifty."

"You better not. She won't even admit she's in her forties." Her aunt looked out over the crowd. "Look at her working the crowd. Your mother thrives on the limelight."

Bridget watched her mother talking to the mayor's wife and gesturing more than once directly at her. Bridget could only imagine what she was telling the mayor's wife about her high-fashion model daughter. And that feeling of euphoria wafted over her for her success and accomplishments. She'd parlayed her beauty into a successful career that afforded her all the best things in life. Money, beautiful clothes, fast cars, fast men—an exhilarating life moving at 180 mph.

There was one niggling little doubt. The Richard

Lawrence contract. She was counting on this lucrative job to power her into the big-time. With the promise of that contract and against her CPA's warnings, she'd bought herself a beautiful Manhattan loft and almost bankrupted herself. But the money was as good as in her pocket.

Her thoughts were interrupted when she saw Matt. And she was once again bowled over by her sudden visceral reaction to him. He stood near a table alone as if he, too, were looking for an opportunity to talk to her.

He seemed to loom larger than life, a gorgeous, sexy mass of brains and brawn. He cut a nice figure in his very proper open-necked dress shirt and sport coat, very professor-like. If she knew Matt, she was sure that's exactly what he was going for. Matt always planned even the minutest detail. Every line of his body projected a calm, cool, collected attitude as if he observed everything from afar and analyzed it behind those warm, intelligent eyes.

"Aunt Ida, could you excuse me?"

"Certainly, but you'd better get back here to help me blow out the candles before they set off the sprinkler alarm."

Bridget chuckled and gave her aunt a quick hug. "Happy birthday, Aunt Ida. You're not getting older, you're getting better."

"Ah, posh. Better than what?"

Bridget moved away from the table flashing her aunt a grin. She searched the crowd again and then she saw Matt. Even though she'd been blindsided at the limo, all the air rushed out of her lungs once again. Something unspoken passed between them when his eyes met hers, reminiscent of the stunned few moments before her mother came pounding down the stairs and ruined everything on that fateful day.

Yet when she met his eyes, she experienced the same intense feelings filling up her chest. She could almost feel his mouth on hers, his warm breath, the contours of his body pressed to hers. She really couldn't leave here until she experienced all that Matt had to offer.

Matt moved away from the table and started toward her. Riveted to the floor, she was thankful he was coming to her. She wasn't sure how well her legs would hold up. When he reached her where she stood in the middle of the room, he smiled in such a sweet, adorable way, she melted inside.

"Matthew Fox, you've grown up," she said, reaching out her hands. He took her hands in his, surprising her by kissing the back of her hands, his fine, full lips moving across her knuckles. She shivered.

"Looks like you've gotten everything you dreamed of," he said.

"I did. Did you?"

"Almost. I've landed a research professorship at MIT at the Fibers and Polymers Laboratory in the Department of Mechanical Engineering, but I'm angling for a tenure track position there."

"To do what?"

"Teach in my field, textile engineering."

"Textile engineering? Like in clothing?"

"Yes."

"I see. So you said you were a research professor. What do you research?"

"Synthesis and development of novel barrier materials including copolymers, inorganic-organic nanocomposites and electrostatic nanolayer assemblies. I also create mathematical modeling of transport phenomena in complex protective clothing ensembles."

"Whoa. Beyond my understanding."

"Sorry. I study ways to make protective clothing safer."

"Does all that technical jargon mean you make cloth?"

"I hold a lot of patents for uses in many applications and just recently I've stumbled across a synthetic cloth that's lightweight, durable and really soft."

"I'd really like to see it sometime."

"Sure. I'm not really sure what I'm going to do with it at this point. I want it to be useful. How long are you going to be in Cambridge? Do you have time to catch up with an old friend?"

"I've got to get back to New York tomorrow for a shoot, but I could come over after Aunt Ida's party for a little while if you like."

"That would be great."

"MIT. Your parents must be so proud of you."

He shrugged and smiled. "Sure, I guess."

The humbleness of his answer surprised her. In the wake of all his achievements, she'd expected that maybe Matt had changed. But looking up into those warm eyes, she could see that Matt had stayed true to himself in the years they'd been away from each other. Could she say the same thing about herself?

"How are your parents?"

"My folks sold me the house and moved to Arizona to help with my mom's arthritis. You know, the dry heat and all."

"Bridget." Her mother appeared, her eyes darting to Matt. "There you are. I want you to meet the mayor's wife. She's just dying to hear about your latest trip to Paris." She turned her focus on Matt. "You will excuse us," she said and she didn't wait for his answer.

It felt like déjà vu all over again as her mother pulled her away from Matt and toward the mayor's wife. A frisson of impatience at her mother's high-handedness rippled through her before she squashed it. Her mother had been the driving force to get her where she was today. She should be grateful. Besides, the Paris fashions were to die for.

She gave Matt an apologetic look. *I'll see you tonight,* she mouthed.

He nodded and that intangible electricity flowed over her like mist. She intended to *see, feel* and *taste* all of him and settle once and for all her burning curiosity to find out just how it would be to make love to Dr. Matthew Fox.

2

HE SIMPLY FELT DAZZLED as he watched Bridget move away from him. He rolled his shoulders in the sport coat and retreated from the center of the floor. There had been so many times when he'd stared down at her picture on the cover of a magazine. He'd never expected to be this close to her again.

He stood on the fringes of the ballroom where he felt secure watching the people socialize and party.

"Why aren't you out there, Matt?"

He turned to find Bridget's aunt standing next to him. She offered him a flute of champagne.

"I feel more comfortable here, Mrs. Jenkins."

"When are you going to stop calling me Mrs. Jenkins, Matt? It would seem after living next door for so long and being friends with Bridget you could call me Aunt Ida. If you don't, I'm going to start calling you Dr. Fox."

Matt's chest swelled as he accepted the flute of champagne and chuckled. "You leave me no choice, Aunt Ida."

"That's better."

"Bridget looks good. Happy."

"I suspect she is, but I'm worried about her. She travels so much, parties with her New York friends and spends her money so lavishly. I had no need of this grand party, but she insisted."

"You deserve one grand party, Mrs....Aunt Ida, after all the good things you did for her. She didn't forget about you."

"Comes from good stock." Aunt Ida smiled, but she watched her niece with an anxious eye. "I wouldn't protest if it was only one grand party, but she's taken me and her mother to Milan, Paris and even Tokyo. That was a wonderful trip. I do have to thank her for showing me some of the world."

"I don't think you should worry. She looks like she's at the top of her game."

"That's Bridget for you."

"Her mother hasn't changed much." Matt winced. "Sorry, that was out of line."

"No, you're correct. Her mother is caught up with what Bridget does, not who she is."

"Do you think that'll ever change?"

"I don't know. Maybe someday." Her aunt smiled at Matt. "Bridget's asked about you over the years, but first you were at Auburn for college, then you settled in North Carolina. It's very good that you've finally come home."

"It feels really good to be home."

He took a sip of champagne and watched Bridget mingle with one guest after another while listening to Aunt Ida expound on her trips with Bridget. Finally her mother took her aside and it appeared to Matt as if they were arguing.

"I CAN'T BELIEVE that you'll only be here one more night and you won't come home. Your father misses you." The soft whine in her mother's voice surprised Bridget. It wasn't often she was asked to stay with her parents when she was in town. In fact, her mother preferred that Bridget stay with her aunt.

Bridget kept her comments about her father to herself. He was her stepfather and her mother had married him when Bridget had been two. Her biological father had been killed in a car accident.

The truth was her stepfather barely noticed she was alive. He was a Harvard professor and spent all his time with his students and his research. Her mother hated it, but would never admit it to Bridget. She'd had to plead to get him to come to her sister's party tonight.

"I'd like your company, then I can give you a ride to the airport tomorrow." Her mother beseeched her with her eyes. It was very odd.

"Is there something wrong?" Bridget asked. They never talked about her mother's marriage. Her mother covered up her unhappiness and Bridget was sure that was why her mother preferred her to stay at her aunt's house.

"No. Why would there be something wrong?"

"Because you're acting strange."

Her mother huffed. "Now, I'm strange."

"I didn't say you were strange. I said…never

mind. I told you that I promised Matt I would catch up with him, Mom."

"Some boy you haven't seen in twelve years is more important than your family? I'm your mother, Bridget."

Guilt cut through her. It was true. She hadn't spent a lot of time with her mother this year. "I'll come home with you tonight. I'll have to tell Matt. Excuse me."

She found him standing close to the kitchen door talking to one of the busboys who had been clearing the tables.

She only caught the tail end of the conversation and overheard the name David Backer as the boy took one look at her and hightailed it back to the kitchen.

Matt turned toward her. "You scared him off."

"I'm not that scary."

"Yes, you are. Scary beautiful, so that any man has to get up his courage just to look at you, let alone talk to you."

"You're talking to me."

"I'm immune. I knew you when you were a bratty kid and a petulant teenager."

"I wasn't petulant."

"You were, too. Petulant, mischievous, reckless and a rule breaker of the highest order."

"And you were none of those things. Solid, smart and reserved. Leave it to you to ignore champagne, caviar and a jamming DJ to talk to a kid about David Backer. Who is he?"

"David Backer or the guy I was talking to?"

"Both."

"David Backer founded the lab I work in and the kid is a student in one of my summer classes at MIT. He's working here to make money to go back to school in the fall."

Bridget shook her head in resignation. "Let's go on the patio," she said, slipping her arm through his. "They have a beautiful garden here. Almost as beautiful as my mother's."

They passed through the open French doors. The cooling breeze of the early summer night touched her shoulders and made her shiver slightly. Matt immediately took off his sport coat and draped the fabric across her shoulders. His hands lingered there, making her shiver all over again as a response to the warmth of his jacket and the pressure of his hands. He was a solid presence at her back and so tall. As kids, she'd been taller than him for the longest time. Then, when he'd been thirteen, he'd started to grow and surpassed her in no time. It was the same year he'd begun to lift weights. He was sick of being pushed around by guys who thought he was easy pickings.

"You're here to tell me that you can't come over tonight. Break bad news surrounded by beauty. Good call."

Matt was so damn smart that it intimidated her sometimes. "My mother insists I go home with her and have some family time and I wanted a private place to tell you. If I remember correctly, parties are not your forte."

"Is she still running your life?"

Bridget turned to face him. "That's not very fair, Matt. She helped me get to where I am."

He gently guided her away from the French doors and down the steps into a shadowed courtyard. "Look, I'm sorry. Residual resentment. That was out of line. She doesn't like me. She never did."

"Why do you say that?"

"Do you have any idea how many times I called you that whole year after your party?"

"You called my house?"

"Countless times. Your mother told me you were busy or not at home. I gave up."

"She never told me you called. Not once. I thought you regretted…"

Matt didn't respond immediately as he stared down into her face. *No, stared isn't the right word,* she mused. She felt more as if he was studying her. Matt's dark, exotic eyes sent chills through her. Observant was the word that came to mind. He seemed to be investigating every angle and plane of her face as if she were a very interesting science project.

The birds and the bees kind of science project.

"Never." His voice was rough and achingly raw. "I'll admit that after that great kiss, our relationship had to change, but not once did I regret knowing you, Bridget."

She met his intense gaze head-on, got lost in the swirling brown of his eyes, the tipped corners. She reached out and touched the tantalizing curve of one eye.

"I'm so thankful because your opinion means a great deal to me, mister."

She took his hand and led him over to a stone bench set near bottle-green hedgerows. The smell of night blooming jasmine permeated the air with a subtle scent. A perfect setting for a tête-à-tête.

"So tell me about your life in New York. Is it what you expected when you were dreaming about modeling and I tried to focus attention on your math problems?"

"I had to work really, really hard."

Matt laughed. "So it is a myth that models just stand around and look pretty."

"A big one. Sómetimes I go through a grueling eight-hour day, have to run home, change and zip off to a nightclub opening or an editorial bash a magazine is throwing. Everything at the agency is managed, from my bookings to my social life. It can get exhausting."

"But I see in your eyes that you love it."

"I do. The attention is fun, especially when people recognize me and say hi. I covet the clothes and love the glamour. Oh, and the money is phenomenal."

"That's clear from this bash. It looks like you brought New York to Cambridge."

"I booked the hottest club disc jockey in New York. That was no easy feat. I had to call in a few favors. My mother helped with the food and decorations. She's very good at throwing a party. Now, how about you Dr. Fox? Making cloth. That excites me."

"It excited me, too. I was trying to make a synthetic fiber to be useful in maybe sports or the military and ended up with this delicately spun stuff. Almost like silk, but more durable and really soft."

"I've got to see this cloth. Aunt Ida said you went to Auburn. Did you get your Ph.D. there, too?"

"My masters and Ph.D."

"I couldn't imagine that, Matt. I never got to college. I feel odd sometimes since so many models manage to do both, but I was focused and intent on my career, never doubting that I would make it."

"You were always that kind of person. Saw what you wanted and went for it."

"Truth or dare, Matt."

"Truth. The last time you dared me, I got myself into hot, hot water."

"You really don't understand this game. Truth can do that, too."

"I considered the possibility, but truth doesn't require some embarrassing action."

"If you didn't know me back then, would you want to be friends with me now?"

"Definitely not."

She laughed and bumped his shoulder. "Be serious, Matt."

"For a kids' game of Truth or Dare?"

"Okay, forget Truth or Dare. Just answer the question."

"A lot of time has passed and we've been out of touch. Our lives are at opposite sides of the spectrum. I guess the truthful answer is that all you've achieved is not who you are, so I'd say yes. I would want to know you now, the woman who can make a man drop to his knees."

"It's really too bad I can't come over tonight."

He nodded. "It was great to see you, though. Maybe we can hook up next time you're in town."

"Definitely. I'm not sure when that will be. I've got something in the works that may keep me busy for a while."

"The price of fame."

"A high price," she said, smiling.

He backed away from her as if he were reluctant to leave. When he reached the stairs, he turned away from her and climbed them.

"Matt," Bridget called, starting after him.

Without thought she ran up to him and threw her arms around his neck. In that moment, peacefulness settled over her, as if she were swimming in a deep, warm pool. She held on to him tightly and experienced joy—an instantaneous feeling. It was like the warmth of homecoming, impossibly poignant and completely wonderful. Bridget could barely breathe.

Matt's arms slipped around her hesitantly; he was clearly as surprised as she. Then his hold tightened and it felt so good to be hugged against him. She released him and looked up into his smiling handsome face and felt a sizzle along her nerve endings, something electric.

She grabbed a handful of his shirt in her fist, getting serious fast.

She already knew firsthand that Matt was a good

kisser, but the thought that he may have gotten better over twelve years almost made her knees buckle.

She could almost thank all those women he'd practiced on. Almost.

She used his collar to guide him down to her waiting lips. He was gently demanding, his big hands having moved from her shoulders down her arms, then back up again to finally cup her cheeks.

It seemed to her that he held her as if she were made of spun glass, fragile and ethereal as if at any moment he would wake and she would disappear; he kissed her as if she was the only woman in the world that mattered.

Thinking about how it would be if she was ever lucky enough to get this close to Matt again filled her fantasies to bursting. She wasn't disappointed as she sank into his mouth, her hand resting against the curve of muscle right below his heart.

Threading her fingers through the thick, silky hair at the nape of his neck, she felt the kiss slide from warm into hot and devouring. Her tongue swept into his mouth and tangled with his tongue, and she tasted the pure, unadulterated sensuality that was so much a part of him. She shivered, unable to stop the slow, sultry ache spreading through her belly.

He moved closer, one of his hands shifting to cup the back of her head to hold her in place, and she felt a low growl rumble up from his chest. He slanted his mouth across hers and took control of the embrace.

Presumptuous and dominant, he kissed her with potent male heat. Branded her with the strength and depth of his passion. Excited her with the heated stroke of his hand on her bare back underneath the sport coat, and the promise of forbidden, illicit pleasures to come.

When he broke the kiss, she sighed softly. "Twelve years was way too long to wait for a kiss like that."

"And how. When I got your aunt's invitation this morning, I wondered if you even remembered me."

"I remembered you. I couldn't ever forget how good you were to me. I've missed that terribly." She brushed his face with the backs of her fingers. "We can't really deny this, can we?"

"No, but I'm not sure we can do anything about it."

"You're not interested?"

"Yes. I'm definitely interested, but, be serious, Bridget, you live in the fast lane and I very much like the slow lane. I don't think it would be a good idea," he said, his eyes apologetic.

"I'm sorry, Matt."

"I think you're very focused on your career and there's probably very little room for anyone else. Truthfully, I don't want to take the risk. It hurt last time, Bridget. Even though I have an explanation as to why you never called me back. It still hurt."

"I understand. It was very good to see you."

"You, too."

He disappeared through the French doors and Bridget blinked back sudden tears. The one person on this planet she would never want to hurt was Matt. But he had been—through her mother's callous actions. Now Bridget wished she had made some attempt to contact him, though maybe deep down she realized that a romantic relationship wouldn't work and they could both end up getting hurt.

Matt was right, she was very focused on her career and although she wanted to satisfy her curiosity about how hot Matt was in bed, she wouldn't.

It was safer this way.

For both of them.

FRIDAY MORNING after her plane landed, Bridget slipped out of the cab she'd hailed, directing the driver to Park Avenue South where CosmoCity Models had their agency offices. She was right on time for her ten o'clock appointment with her agent. She made her way to the twenty-second floor and entered through a glass door into the stylish reception area.

On her flight and all the way from the airport she couldn't stop thinking about Matt. She tried to relegate him to the past, but she couldn't seem to. She wanted to see him again, she couldn't deny it. If only she hadn't kissed him again. Remembering his mouth, the heat of him, made her attraction to him intensify.

The receptionist waved at her as she walked by. Making her way into the back offices, Bridget passed by the boards, a wall of plastic pockets housing hundreds of composites of all the agency's working models. The boards were separated into different categories—the high board where supermodels commanded the largest fees with recognizable names and faces; the working board for commercial models who worked steadily in catalog, advertising, television and editorial; and the sophisticated woman board where older models' bookings included catalog and advertising featuring young moms.

Glancing at them briefly, she hoped that her composite would soon move from commercial to the high board with the anticipated contract for major designer Richard Lawrence soon to be announced. He'd picked her portfolio out of many that the agency had sent him and she'd gone on a go-see two weeks ago. He'd been thrilled with her look.

She turned away from the boards and continued to her agent's beautifully appointed office with a prime view of New York.

Leslie Dawson looked up as Bridget walked in. "Right on time, Bridget. Have a seat."

Okay, she was brisk. That wasn't a good sign. No questions about her aunt's birthday or her trip to Cambridge. The one thing she could be sure of with Leslie was that the woman was straightforward and never glossed over anything.

"We got the contract from Richard Lawrence."

A sense of accomplishment washed over her and, she had to admit, relief. This Woman of Substance campaign to launch new classic, hip clothes could be her ticket to the big-time. "That's great, Leslie. When do I…"

"Bridget. The offer is for Tracy Morgan."

Everything inside her clenched. Young, perky Tracy Morgan, who seemed to be getting every break that came along recently. "Tracy? I didn't know she was up for this job. I thought they wanted me."

"Seems Richard changed his mind. They want a younger woman, early twenties."

Bridget was so stunned, adrenaline flowed into her bloodstream. With buying the loft, this came as a big ugly shock.

"You haven't been earning as well as you had in the past, Bridget. There was talk of placing you on the sophisticated woman board, but I pointed out that you have several covers in your portfolio and should be allowed to continue on the commercial board for now."

Trying to quell a swell of panic, she said, "The sophisticated woman board. You mean the washed-up board."

"We don't call it that."

"That's what it is," Bridget insisted.

"That's not what it is. Young mothers are commanding a large segment of the market now and since you're a savvy businesswoman…"

"Yes, I know what that means. They have more buying power."

"Everyone has to adjust for market trends—designers, agents and models. We all want a piece of the pie. You're now in your late twenties and have been with CosmoCity for ten years. Modeling doesn't last forever."

"I know that, and I'm not quite ready to give up yet."

"That's a good attitude. It's not a bleak outlook by any means. You know how this business works. Your look just wasn't right for Lawrence. I'm going to contact Maggie Winterbourne's camp. I heard they are keeping a lucrative campaign under wraps. Let's see what I can find out."

Bridget cleared her throat, trying to dislodge the tight lump there. Maggie Winterbourne was the cream of the designer crop. Getting a contract there would boost her career and her ego, which was quite bruised right now. "What's the next step?"

"Your contract with Kathleen Armstrong comes up for renewal next month. It's to your advantage that you were never typecast. You've also carried more than one contract at a time. Unusual for this business. That could very well happen again. It'll take patience and time. I'll contact Kathleen's rep and get a new contract negotiated."

"Kathleen isn't on the same playing field as Richard Lawrence and certainly not Maggie Winterbourne."

"I know you're disappointed, Bridget. I don't have any bookings for you next week. Why don't you take some time off and rest."

"You're aware I gave up the lease on my apartment and bought a loft. I have to be out of my apartment by Friday. I don't want to rest, Leslie. I need to work."

"I understand, but worrying isn't going to make it happen and it'll show on your face. If I get any work for you, I'll call. I'm on your side, Bridget."

"I know you are, and thanks."

BRIDGET ENTERED the photographer's studio to see Tracy Morgan posing for the camera. She couldn't help wishing the little contract-stealing wench would trip and break her ankle. No, make that her neck.

She went into the dressing room and came face-to-face with Kathleen Armstrong.

Kathleen's eyes widened in confusion. "Bridget? I'm surprised to see you."

Bridget set down her bag on the makeup table. "Why would that be? I've been booked for this shoot for some time. Has something happened?"

Kathleen walked over to the door and closed it. "I guess the word didn't get to you. I'll have to speak to my assistant. I don't need you today."

Bridget stared at Kathleen, alarm paralyzing her for an instant. With her heart hammering hard against her breastbone, she said, "I see."

The significance of what was finally going on penetrated. "Look, I want to get my bad news all in one gulp. Did you give this job to Tracy?"

"Yes, I did. I've been thinking that I need a younger model. It's nothing against you, Bridget, but you know how the world works."

Swallowing hard, she said, "Youth and beauty." She also knew exactly what Kathleen was going to say next.

"Right. I'm afraid that I won't be renewing your contract, as well. Of course, you'll be compensated for the rest of your current one."

Even though she expected the words, her heart stammered in her chest, a frisson of unease shivered up her spine and her legs suddenly felt weak. "I figured that part out." Bridget gritted her teeth and reached out her hand. "Thanks for everything, Kathleen."

"You're a very professional person, Bridget. I've had models scream at me when I fired them."

Feeling as if there was a scream climbing up her throat, Bridget nodded, turned and left.

"BRIDGET, I WARNED YOU about spending so lavishly," Naomi Carlyle, her CPA, said, sliding her report over to Bridget across Bridget's coffee table.

Bridget looked through all the numbers and the accounts and sighed, her heart heavy. "So I'm broke."

Naomi's expressive green eyes filled with sympathy. "Pretty close to it. You're going to have to be very careful with your spending."

The sympathy only made Bridget more determined to weather this and turn it around somehow. Frustration gripped her hard, giving her tone a sharp edge she rarely used. "Oh, damn."

"What?"

"The loft. I still have to be out of my apartment by Friday."

"I'm so sorry." Naomi's serious eyes captured Bridget's. "I have an idea for your loft, though."

"Please, anything that will help."

"You could rent it out furnished. Just move your furniture into the loft. Do you have someone you can stay with?"

"Yes, as a matter of fact, I do. I have an aunt in Cambridge."

"It's not ideal, if you're trying to get modeling jobs, but doable. The drive is only about three and a half hours."

Bridget got up and paced to the windows that held a nice, if not exceptional view of the city. The loft she'd bought did have an exceptional view and someone else was going to enjoy it. Her nerves shot after the day's revelations, she leaned her head against the glass. "That's not everything."

Naomi groaned from her seat on the couch.

"I just threw a very lavish party for my aunt."

"Then, my friend, you'd better get yourself a job, pronto."

Those words echoed in Bridget's head the following morning. Unable to stay still, she paced from room to room. She needed to find a job and she wasn't sure after what happened with Kathleen if she still had an agency to go to. But that blow would be too much to take right now. She'd face that on Monday when she had to face moving into a loft she wasn't going to be able to live in and finding a tenant.

She wasn't used to money problems. Her mother had provided for her until she was working on her own. But she couldn't ask her mother for money. She couldn't let on that she was broke and her career was on a downslide. Bridget didn't believe for one moment that she couldn't get herself back on track. It would take work, but she wasn't afraid to get her hands dirty.

She was afraid of only one thing.

Failure.

3

BRIDGET FINISHED UP her fiftieth lap across her aunt's pool, trying to release some of her pent-up anxiety about how she was going to pay the mounting bills from her aunt's party. She'd arrived last night after a week of taking care of moving her furniture into her new loft, finding a tenant to fill the space and pestering Leslie for work.

Nothing had materialized and Bridget was in just as much financial hot water as she had been a week ago. She chafed at the inactivity and her aunt, tired of her pacing, had told her to get into her swimsuit and release some of the tension.

It was just now that she was beginning to realize how much she missed that special, nothing-to-hide friendship she'd shared with Matt.

With that in mind, she got out of the pool and headed to the patio where she slipped into the hot tub. Nothing like a soak in hot water to soothe her muscles and mellow her out.

She closed her eyes to shut out the brightness of the early-morning summer sunshine when she heard a lawn mower in the distance. Bridget got out of the tub and walked over to the lounge chair, reaching for her towel. While she dried the excess water from her hair and body, the lawn mower sputtered and died. Dropping the wet towel onto the lounge, she donned a hot pink cover-up over her swimsuit.

Walking to the edge of the patio, she shielded her eyes against the hot sun, but Matt wasn't in his backyard.

She walked around the side of her aunt's house and finally saw Matt. He knelt on his front lawn, the lawn mower turned upside down.

He had on a white muscle T-shirt and a pair of black athletic shorts that showed off his sleek thighs. Bridget found her gaze inexorably drawn to him, mesmerized by the way the muscles in his arms, across his back and down his thighs rippled and bunched as he worked on the mower.

He was a gorgeous, earthy, sexy man—even when he was covered in grass and sweat—and her attraction to him was impossible to ignore, no matter how hard she tried. So, she looked her fill, let her mind wander down dangerous roads, and imagined seductive scenarios that made her heart race and her body ache to be near him. But those fantasies dancing in her mind inevitably turned to a soul-deep wanting.

It was then that Matt looked up and saw her. She caught the surprise in his eyes, then a fleeting glimpse of the heat and hunger that smoldered in his amber eyes.

"Hey," he called, "I thought you went back to New York."

She came forward until she reached him. "I did."

He fiddled with the blade of the mower. "For a visit?"

"Not exactly." Her voice must have given her away because Matt stopped fiddling with the machinery and looked at her.

"Are you all right?"

The concern in his voice brought strong emotion swirling inside her, making her long for simpler days where nothing existed but their special friendship.

But the real world did exist, and hers consisted of a life that was fraught with serious problems, ones she was determined to overcome. A life Matt didn't understand here in the small town of Cambridge. A life she'd fought for and sacrificed so much for. Her accomplishments made her who she was. If she wasn't a model, what was she?

Knowing all this didn't stop Bridget from wanting more of Matt Fox, more of the emotional connection she experienced only when she was with him. Beyond their physical attraction, he made her feel, and it had been a long time, if ever, since anyone had touched her heart so profoundly.

"I will be okay."

"Is there anything I can do to help?"

"Not unless you've got a job in your back pocket."

"You don't have a job?"

"I lost a couple of contracts and my bookings have dried up. It happens in this business. I still have an agent, so I'm sure things will pick up soon." Her stomach clenched just saying the words as her confidence wavered a little.

Matt looked deep into her eyes and seemed to want to reach out, but stopped. "I'm sure everything will work out." His voice was low and soothing.

"Thanks for the vote of confidence."

He flipped the lawn mower over and looked at it, deep in thought. "At least it died after I finished the lawn, but I still have your aunt's to do."

"Can I help you?"

His eyes widened and he looked down at her hands, then her attire. "With the mower?"

"Sure."

"How about you go get my toolbox for me in the garage? It's on the workbench—and grab a couple of rags for me to wipe my hands."

"I'm not afraid to get my hands dirty, Matt."

He smiled. "I'll do the dirty work."

"I bet you do dirty really well," she said, unable to resist the pull of attraction.

He slanted her a sidelong glance that packed a provocative punch, shifting as if he was suddenly uncomfortable in his shorts. "I get by. Just go get the toolbox."

As she walked away, she could feel the heat of Matt's gaze on her backside, and it took every ounce of willpower she possessed not to glance over her shoulder to look at him, to let him know in a single adoring glance how much she wanted him—ached for him, desired him—despite the way things had played out at her aunt's birthday party. She would respect Matt's wishes to keep her attraction under control. The thought of potentially hurting him again made her resolve tighten.

Once inside the garage, she focused on the toolbox like a lifeline. Bridget scanned the area. It was neat and tidy, everything in place. Walking between a brown sedan and a car covered with a dust cloth, Bridget spied the toolbox and the rags on a workbench nearby. Stopping in front of the workbench, her curiosity got the better of her. She lifted the dust cloth and looked underneath. She found a gleaming midnight-blue vintage Porsche coupe. She thought it was criminal to keep a car like that hidden in the garage on a day like today. It stirred her blood to imagine being in the smooth leather bucket seat flying down the road at an exhilarating speed.

She picked up the toolbox, snatched up a couple of rags and made her way back to Matt.

She set the box near him and knelt back in the grass. "You have a sports car under wraps in there. Is there a wild man hidden somewhere inside you, Matt?"

"It's not my car. I'm just storing it for my dad." Matt opened the toolbox and pulled out a screwdriver.

"You have to drive it," she exclaimed. "You can't leave a beautiful car like that idle. It'll ruin it."

"No, I don't leave it idle. I drive it every week. On Saturdays as a matter of fact." He took out the screws and removed the casing of the small motor.

"I don't know why I was worried. Of course, you do. You plan everything."

His shoulders stiffened and he set the casing on

the grass beside him. "There's nothing wrong with planning ahead. It's like a compass that keeps you moving forward."

She watched his emotional barriers rise and remembered how stubborn Matt could be, and how set in his ways. But instead of being bothered, she felt as if she'd rediscovered a pearl that she'd lost a long time ago. "True, but if you follow the compass, you might miss a particularly beautiful view and lose a special experience you could have had."

"Hand me that wrench," he asked, his hands now covered in gunk and grease.

She reached into the box, grabbed the tool and handed it to him.

"I don't think it's smart to go off without a road map," he said.

The irritated tone in his voice was another pearl that she loved discovering. His prickliness was a defense mechanism. She wanted the true Matt to shine again and the thought sent pure joy jetting into her system. "When I was in Italy last year, there were plenty of brochures in the hotel for all the usual tourist attractions, but I didn't want to see Italy through the eyes of a brochure. I wanted to see it through *my* eyes. I got off the beaten track and I'll admit it—I got lost. But I ended up walking into this beautiful garden to ask for directions. I stumbled onto a wedding. Those gracious people invited me in. I drank Chianti, sang, ate, danced and had a grand time. That sure beats looking at some old ruins I could see anytime I pleased."

She watched a play of rueful emotions chase across his face. "I would have gone to the ruins." He removed the carburetor and sat cross-legged on the lawn.

"I also got this cover-up in a little bazaar I stumbled across while exploring." She reached out and touched his arm, grinning wryly. "So next time you go to Italy, Matt, try to get yourself lost."

Gesturing toward the toolbox, he scowled.

When she followed his pointing finger to a piece of wire, she snagged it.

"I've never been to Italy," he said.

Her startled gaze cut sharply to him. "Really?"

"I like it just fine in Cambridge." He threaded the wire into the part he held in his hand.

"That's too bad. I'm lucky that traveling is part of my job. I'd think nothing of being in London one day and then Paris the next."

Matt was silent for a moment. "Why don't you come with me later for a drive?"

"I'd love to."

"It's pretty."

"What?"

"That cover-up thing." He wiped his hands on one of the rags she'd brought and lifted the insert away to reveal the bottom of the toolbox. He reached for an aerosol can with *carb cleaner* printed on the side. He sprayed a steady stream into the carburetor.

"Thanks." Not wanting to leave, she started, "Uh, speaking of cover-ups. How did you get into textile engineering?"

"The textile industry is one of the largest in America, producing everything from the fabric used in the clothes we wear to the plastic in IV tubes. I liked being part of an industry so vital and important to our society's needs."

"Interesting how we are connected in what we do for jobs. You make the stuff I wear. It's symbiotic."

Matt nodded, finishing up with the carburetor. Setting it back into the engine assembly, he screwed the bolts into the casing. "I never really thought about it. But you're right."

"And the fabric you invented. Have you decided what to do about it?"

"Not yet. Would you like to see it?"

"Yes, very much."

He wiped his hands again, putting the can back in the toolbox and setting the insert back in place. He closed the lid. Standing, he pulled the cord to the lawn mower and it started right up.

He smiled at Bridget over the noise, before cutting the engine.

"Let's get everything put away and I'll show you. I'll mow your aunt's lawn later."

He pushed the mower back to the garage while Bridget followed with the toolbox.

"I'm going to clean up a little before going in the house. You can unveil the car if you like."

"I would like to see all of it."

He walked out of the garage and Bridget pulled the cover off the car, getting a thrill out of the sleek design and gauging how fast it would go.

When she was finished, she went looking for

Matt. She heard running water on the side of the house. She headed in that direction and stopped dead in her tracks as if she'd hit a brick wall.

Matt was using the hose high over his head like a shower. She watched in fascination as the droplets slid tantalizingly over the molded contours of his pectoral muscles, slipping down his smooth chest, down over the rippling strength of his stomach and disappeared into the waistband of his dark shorts. Her eyes remained there, her pulse jumping in rapid succession, her breathing increasing into little puffs, desire curling inside of her, tightening like a vise.

From his rumpled hair and striking amber eyes to that lean, honed body she'd imagined naked and aroused, he exuded raw sex appeal and brought her feminine instinct to keen awareness as no other man had.

He turned his head to look at her, his eyes locking with hers across the short expanse. There was unmistakable desire there, but there was distance, too.

A clear message that said, look but don't touch. Matt was fast becoming a reckless addiction. She ached to caress all that slick, glistening flesh.

But she knew why he had that wary look in his eyes. She'd inadvertently broken his trust and no matter how it happened, it had happened. Without mutual trust, they would only have *hot* sex between them and while physical attraction was what seared through her now, it wasn't enough of a foundation to build the kind of relationship she knew Matt would demand.

She wasn't exactly sure she could handle that kind of relationship anyway. She wouldn't stay in boring Cambridge for very long. Soon she would get another contract and go back to New York. She could still reach the pinnacle of the success she craved, if she worked hard enough. But, even that thought didn't cool her ardor at all.

Matt turned off the hose and together they went into the house. When he'd changed clothes, he handed her a bolt of cloth. "What do you think?"

Bridget peeled the cloth away from the bolt. It felt like silk and velvet had melded, so soft against the palm of her hand. "This is gorgeous. I bet you'd feel almost naked wearing it. Almost naked. Now there's a name."

"It gets my attention."

"I'm no expert, but I think this would make beautiful lingerie."

"Really."

"Yes, sensual against the body."

Matt rubbed the back of his neck. "Lingerie. Not exactly up my alley."

"No, I would guess not."

"Maybe you could take it and work some of your clothing magic on it. Give me some ideas?"

"You mean designing something?"

"Sure. How else will I know what to do with it? I'm an engineer, Bridget. I'm into the science of it and practical uses. Lingerie isn't exactly practical."

"I don't know. I'm not really a designer."

"You make great stuff. Give it a try. For me."

"Okay, I'll see what I can come up with."

"Why don't you go get changed and I'll get the car ready."

She shook her head. "Matt, you are so practical."

WHEN SHE GOT BACK, he put the key in the passenger door lock and twisted. The locks popped.

Bridget made no move to get into the car. He realized how close he was standing to her. For a smart guy, he had underestimated his attraction to her. It was like fighting through water to resist the temptation of touching her. He knew she wanted him and that only added to the hot need that spiraled inside him. All he had to do was move a fraction of an inch and he could kiss her.

She waited for his move, caught and held in the same electric current as he was. He could see the knowledge in her eyes that a strong attraction like this wouldn't so easily be dismissed. He should send her packing, but now that he knew she was in trouble, he couldn't.

He cleared his throat and said, "Let's go." Breathing a sigh of relief, or was that regret, he slid down into the seat, taking up a whole lot of space in the intimately compact interior. Only the console between them kept their thighs from touching.

He buckled his seat belt, she did the same, and then he turned the key. The car rumbled to life beneath him. The powerful engine tickled the backs of his thighs where they met luxurious leather, vibrating down his calf and all the way to his toes. He moved his hand to the gearshift and shifted into reverse.

He slid the windows down to air out the stuffy car.

"Let's leave the windows down, the breeze is wonderful. I love the smell of summer. You don't get this smell in New York. When the city heats up, you don't want to be outside."

He made his way through the city and approached the road that ran along the Charles River, braking to get around cyclists enjoying a beautiful Saturday in June. Kayaks dotted the river along with canoes.

He downshifted through the next corner and the road ran out straight ahead.

"Punch it, Matt."

"That would be speeding."

"Come on, haven't you done anything just a little naughty?"

"No, not really."

"You've got to start living, Matt. Youth doesn't last forever. Believe me. I know firsthand."

Being a levelheaded guy did have its drawbacks as adrenaline kicked through his system. Her playful eyes and impish smile was contagious. He couldn't deny the rush of blood through his veins. Fast cars and fast women. A dangerous combination.

He gave the sports car a little more gas and the engine responded by jumping forward like a horse aching to run.

"Whoo-hoo!" Bridget cried loudly, the sound swallowed by the wind streaming through the windows. He shifted again as the car settled into a running purr.

Her blond hair whipped around her face like

golden silk streamers as she turned her bright eyes to him. She leaned forward and snapped on the radio.

Talking had been difficult over the howl of the wind, but it was now impossible with the throbbing rock that blasted out of the speakers. They rode in companionable silence, something Matt was sure he'd never achieved with any other woman in his life.

When he reached Somerset Park, he pulled into the entrance, paid the entrance fee and parked.

"Bridget, your hair."

She flipped down the visor and peered into the small mirror. "So, it's a tangled mess, it was well worth it." She combed it with her fingers.

She opened the door and swung her legs out. "Tell me I haven't destroyed your fantasies of the perfect woman."

"I know that's not real," he said, watching for her reaction as he, too, pushed out of his seat.

He climbed from the car, and she did the same, shaking her head as she walked toward a picnic table with a spectacular view of the river. "Good for you. Not all guys are like that."

Once he reached the table, he picked up a stone and sent it skipping across the smooth water. "Are you talking from experience?"

She stepped on the seat of the picnic table and settled on the top's flat surface. "Another myth I can dispel. It takes hours to make me look like the perfect woman in pictures. Hours of hair, makeup and wardrobe. I dated this guy that ran screaming from my apartment when he got a load of me in my green herbal mask." She chuckled. "It was pretty funny."

He captured her hand as she self-consciously swept it through her hair. He tightened his fist just slightly. "But I bet it hurt a little, too. I know what it takes to cover up your feelings when you've been unfairly treated because of how you look. I won't judge you, Bridget. Friends don't judge."

Surprise and then tenderness settled in her eyes. She clutched at his hand. "No, they don't. That's why I miss them so much." She swallowed.

Ah, this was much more dangerous than fast cars and fast women. Here it was—the easy camaraderie that was so much a part of their relationship when they'd been young, something so genuine that Matt hungered for that kind of connection again.

Getting involved with her would be a mistake, for both of them. It was all about lifestyle and he knew he couldn't fit into hers.

He gave her hand a squeeze and stepped away. "I should get back. I still have your aunt's lawn to mow. I also have papers to grade."

Suddenly the sound of her cell phone broke the peaceful quiet.

Bridget fished the phone out of her pocket and spoke into it. Matt started to walk away to give her some privacy, but she clutched at his arm to make him stay.

"Tonight? Sure. No. It'll be a great way to network. Count me in."

She finished the call and said excitedly. "That

was my agent on the phone. I've just been invited to a club opening. Very exclusive. I bet there will be plenty of designers there, since it's owned by Maggie Winterbourne."

"You're going back to New York? You just got here last night."

She waved her hand. "No big deal, but transportation is a problem. I really don't want to take the train...." Her gaze went to his father's car. "Matt, how would you like to go to a club opening?"

He put up his hands. "No, Bridget. I'm not driving my father's car to New York City."

"My tenant doesn't take possession of my new loft until Monday. My building has a very secure garage."

"No."

"Matt, please. I don't want to go to this club opening tonight by myself. Why not come and see how the other half lives."

"I'm not interested in the other half. Besides, I have papers to grade and I haven't packed, or planned for a trip."

"Try being spontaneous for once in your life. We don't need bags and you have Sunday to grade papers."

"I need my bags."

"Okay fine. We can go back to your house and pack. Please say yes."

He looked out over the river; his hands slipped into his pockets. "All right."

"YOU'RE WEARING THAT?" Matt asked when Bridget emerged from her bedroom back at her new loft in New York City.

"What? Is it ripped?" She grabbed the hem of the short black pleated skirt to check for holes. The halter couldn't be ripped because it was made of small metal rings sewn closely together.

"I hope not. It won't stay on."

"Oh, Matt. Don't be a prude. I've worn less than this in photo shoots."

"I guess that's what's expected of you."

"You got it. It's all part and parcel of the whole model gig. Show skin and look sexy."

"Sexy? Then I most definitely don't fit in. I think I need help."

"Dress shirt and black slacks are a bit boring, but I do have to say that it looks great on you. Did you bring jeans?"

"No."

"What?"

"I don't have jeans. I don't teach in them. I need to promote a professional image to get tenure. I want to be taken seriously, so no jeans."

"Okay, no jeans. Let's go."

"Are we driving to the opening? I'm not keen about leaving my dad's car…."

"Such a worrywart. We're not going to the opening just yet and, no, we're taking a cab."

"If we're not going to the opening, where are we going?"

"Shopping."

"Shopping?" He sighed. "Fine. It's your world. I'll play in it a little bit longer. But I draw the line at black jackets with chains on them."

"I'm not going to dress you like a biker, for Pete's sake, Matt."

Once in the store, Bridget searched through the trendy T-shirts on a stack in the front. When she came across a silky one made out of chest-hugging material, she handed it to Matt.

He held it up. "It's *hot pink,* Bridget."

"It's not *hot pink.* It's *raspberry.* Geez, Matt, lighten up a little. No one knows you at the club. Why don't you enjoy yourself and step outside the stereotypical professor image for one night. Let your wild man come out."

He rolled his eyes and followed her as she made her way to the jeans rack. She went through them very quickly until she got to a pair by designer Richard Lawrence. Perfect. Classy. She turned to hand the jeans to him, but he was busy looking through the jackets.

"This is nice." He was fingering a black blazer.

Bridget took the jacket out of his hands. "It's cashmere and it'll be perfect with the T-shirt. Aren't you getting hip with the New York glam?"

He gave her a narrow-eyed look. "Oh, you are funny. Where are the dressing rooms?"

"In the back."

She tagged along behind him and he disappeared through a door. While she was waiting, she saw another pair of jeans that might work better. She turned the knob on the door. "Matt, try these on, too."

Her mouth went immediately dry. Matt had pulled on the jeans, but hadn't had a chance to button them and his chest was quite gorgeous and bare. She was close to him, so close she could feel the heat of his body. His warm smile called to her, she stepped forward and the door closed behind her. Pure, undisguised sexual energy crackled between them, a rare and irresistible chemistry that intensified with each moment that passed.

No words were spoken—none were needed—as she lifted a hand and curled her fingers around the nape of his neck. She pulled his lips to hers and kissed him deeply, avidly. His mouth was equally hot and eager, his tongue bold and greedy, consuming her with rich, unadulterated pleasure.

His fingers fluttered along her shoulders. The next thing she knew, her halter top slid down her chest, the metal rings rasping over the taut peaks of her breasts. She moaned softly against his mouth.

He pulled back, his dark eyes caressing every part of her. Her hands swept over the broad expanse of his chest, and she plied his nipples with her thumbs, then strummed her fingers downward to his taut belly. His entire body jerked in response. He slanted his mouth across hers again with a rough growl, his tongue thrusting deep as he pushed her against the dressing room wall.

His free hand roamed up her spine, splaying against the middle of her back and forcing her body to arch into him and her breasts to rub against his chest.

Their bodies were locked tight as he scattered soft, damp, biting kisses along her throat and over the upper slopes of her straining breasts. He circled his tongue around one rigid nipple, blew a hot stream of breath across the peak, then did the same to the other. He lapped at her slowly, licked the taut tips teasingly and nibbled until the madness was too much to bear. Getting one hand free, she grabbed a handful of hair and pressed his parted lips to one aching, tingling crest in silent demand. He obeyed, taking as much of her breast as he could inside the wet warmth of his mouth.

He sucked, and she felt that tugging pulling sensation all the way down to her sex. Reaching down she cupped him in her hand.

"Are you doing okay in there?" A masculine voice said from outside the dressing-room door.

"Damn," Matt whispered shakily.

He looked dazed. Stunned. "We're doing fine," Bridget said, trying not to laugh.

"Got the right size?"

She covered her mouth as their eyes met. Matt's were full of mirth, a lopsided grin on his lips. It took all Bridget had not to groan in frustration. The truth was, Matt felt like exactly the right size and she wanted to experience what she held in her hand up close and personal.

The situation wasn't lost on him as he stared into her eyes.

"Give us a minute. We're almost done," Matt shouted.

They separated and she could see Matt close his eyes with a sigh of relief as the guy walked away.

Bridget reached down and grabbed the ends of her halter and secured it behind her neck. She wondered if Matt had a clue how incredible he looked. She doubted he much cared. Which made him all the sexier to her. Earthy, natural. Raw and showing a crazy side to him she'd never seen.

She paused with her hand on the doorknob. "You'd better get dressed before we lose complete control. Yowza, Dr. Fox. You're the dangerous one."

MATT HELD OUT HIS HAND for Bridget, assisting her from the cab, his stomach clenching at all the reporters. Bridget placed her strappy gold sandal on the curb and emerged from the cab in front of Rags. Camera flashes momentarily blinded him as she automatically posed for the camera.

Another cab pulled up and the cameras swung away from Bridget.

"Is it usually like this?" he asked, thinking that his world was staid and calm compared to this—groups of photographers, journalists and fashionistas milling around, yelling at people as they got out of cabs.

"Pretty much. You get used to it. Asking fashion models to be part of the opening night clientele is common practice in the nightclub business, hopefully garnering instant success. Sex sells everything."

They walked forward and the doorman eyed them both. "Name?"

"Bridget Cole."

He shuffled through the names and said, "Go ahead."

Matt felt rooted to the spot. Why did he agree to this? He felt totally out of his element.

"That's such a hot shirt," a girl with pink hair said as she passed him.

Matt gaped until Bridget took his hand and pulled him forward. "Come on, Matt."

On the way to one of the tables, a man passed Bridget, stopped and came back. "Bridge, honey," he said, giving her one of those hugs that socialites had perfected over the years. "I'm going to St. Barts this weekend, want to come with?"

"I can't, Seth."

"We'll miss you." He walked away as he said it, his eyes going to another woman and he said, "Tanya, honey. St. Barts this weekend?"

"Do you come with to St. Barts, usually?"

"It's a blast when I can go. Seth is harmless, but selfish. Once I went on his private jet and he didn't want to fly me back on time. I had to rebook a commercial and that was a nightmare."

"I bet."

"Aunt Ida met him when we were in Paris and I took her to a nightclub there. She thought he was shallow."

"That's great that you bring your aunt with you when you travel."

"It's too bad she has limited time. She has to work around her schedule at the hospital."

Several people called out Bridget's name and she got pulled in different directions, leaving Matt suddenly on his own. He retreated to the bar, ordered a beer and people-watched. He saw Bridget talking to an elegantly dressed woman near one of the tables full of rowdy people trying to get Bridget's attention. A thought hit him while he watched her network. Bridget needed a job and he needed his fabric marketed. This would work for both of them. He was also swayed by the fact that she was in dire straits. She didn't come right out and say it, but he suspected her troubles were deeper and more overwhelming than she mentioned.

Bridget worked her way through the crowd to him. "Sorry about that."

"Who were you talking to?"

"Maggie Winterbourne. She's a designer I'd give my eyeteeth to work with. A little networking, now a little dancing." She slipped her arm through his, frowning when he didn't budge.

"I'm not really good at dancing," Matt said, his gaze darting to the wall of moving, gyrating humanity in front of him.

"You don't have to be good at it."

She pulled him out to the dance floor, and he moved to the music, while people around him bumped into him in a general frenzy of motion.

After a few minutes he got into it more. Watching Bridget move to the beat of the music inspired him.

Hours later they hailed a cab back to her apartment. She kicked off the gold sandals and dropped her purse and keys on a small table in the foyer. She walked into the kitchen and went to the fridge and grabbed a mineral water. "You want one?"

Matt took in the beautiful loft as he followed Bridget from the foyer through the living quarters. Everything was open except the two bedrooms. Her bare feet flexed on bamboo floors in a kitchen filled with stainless steel appliances, deep wood cabinets and granite countertops.

He nodded, she lobbed the bottle at him and he caught it deftly.

She went into the living room and sat down on her red couch, pushing a button to open the blinds and reveal a view of adjoining buildings and a glimpse of the sky.

"Did you have a good time?"

"It was interesting."

"And you were a really good sport. Thanks for going with me."

"So this is the loft you had to give up?"

"Yes, isn't it gorgeous? I let the promise of the lucrative Richard Lawrence contract seduce me into buying. That old adage is true. Don't count your chickens until they hatch."

"You certainly aren't afraid of risk, Bridget."

"Nope." They clinked bottles. "Some people would call that reckless."

He gestured to the wall behind her, a collage of her magazine covers. Many of the covers he recognized from the days after she'd won the National Pageant. How stupid was he to think he could ever get involved with her as more than a friend. But after that hot and heavy make-out session in the dressing room, how could he resist.

"Quite impressive. Seems too personal to leave here for a tenant."

"I'm proud of them." She shrugged, her eyes going unerringly to his mouth. "Besides, the new tenant is a fashion editor, she won't care. She'll think they're artwork."

"I've been thinking about this ever since I saw you with Maggie Winterbourne. How about you do something with my fabric?"

"What do you mean?"

"It seems perfect to me. You need a job. I need someone to market it and with you being in the fashion biz, you have contacts."

"I don't know, Matt. I could start working again next week, then where would you be?"

"The same place I am now."

Her eyes narrowed. "You're not offering me charity."

"No. You're in a position to help me. I'll name you CEO and with you taking care of the details and putting a public face on the company, I could stay out of it completely."

"So, that's your motivation for not wanting to market it yourself."

"I'm not naive. That fabric is more suited to lingerie and women's clothes than anything else. I don't want to be associated with that kind of thing. Keep my identity a secret." Matt decided that having Bridget as his figurehead was a no-lose proposition. He could make his invention useful without ever blowing his serious-scientist cover and help her in the process.

"Why would you want to do that? You should be proud of your accomplishments."

"In addition to the fact that I need to protect my reputation as a serious scientist, I'm up for that tenure track position. I would rather my research on co-polymers speak for me instead of my invention of a cloth that is used in making baby-doll nightgowns."

"I could use a job. Are you sure, Matt?" Bridget rose.

"I'm sure. Please do this for me."

"I will, then. Thanks for the offer."

He stood up and closed the distance between them. He could smell the sweet scent of woman and perfume that stirred his hormones and devastated his common sense. Reaching out he slipped his index finger beneath her chin and tipped her face up to his, the glow of need mirrored in her eyes, luring him. "I don't think I can resist you anymore, Bridget."

"You could try harder. I don't want to be responsible for you getting hurt again."

"I've tried. I want you," Matt said.

"I want you, too."

"It could get complicated."

She put her fingers over his mouth. "Let's not talk about that, Matt."

"No promises, no problems?" Matt offered.

"And no strings. We can enjoy each other as long as it lasts."

"I haven't been able to stop thinking about you."

She bit her lip and closed her eyes. "Maybe we shouldn't."

"Yes, we should."

"Do you think you can persuade me?"

He brushed his knuckles along her cheek, then cupped her jaw in his hand. "I'm a scientist."

Her brow crinkled in confusion. "What does that have to do with sex?"

"Orgasms after all are just a biological reaction to stimulation."

4

"WHAT...WHAT DID YOU JUST SAY?" she sputtered, a laugh escaping her, totally changing the mood in the room.

"Biology is not funny, Bridget."

This only made her laugh harder and plunk down onto the couch.

Her laughter made him smile. The words came out of his mouth before he could engage the intelligent brain in his very thick head. "Orgasms are biological. Want me to prove it?"

Bridget sat up at this proclamation and stopped laughing. "And exactly what hypothesis would you offer to prove?"

"The main physical changes that occur during a sexual experience are a result of vasocongestion."

"English please."

"It means accumulation of blood in various parts of the body. Muscular tension increases and other changes occur throughout your body."

"Correct me if I'm wrong, but in an experiment, doesn't the scientist perform?"

Matt smiled and then grinned. Maybe biology was a laughing matter after all.

"As a scientist who's very interested in experimenting on you, I can say I definitely can perform."

"Talk, talk, talk. How about some action?"

He hesitated. He recognized the danger, but decided for once in his life he wasn't going to plan this out. The bottom line was he wanted her. He wanted her bad. Common sense and logic paled in comparison to the heady sensation tingling through his body.

"Okay, I guess the subject has to be prepped," Bridget said softly and she unhooked her halter, the rings jingling musically as she dropped it on the floor. She stood up and removed her tight black skirt. Matt swallowed hard. She was clad in nothing but a white transparent thong edged in pink lace.

She reached for his belt buckle and suddenly he had his hands around hers, capturing them.

She raised a brow and tipped her head back. He got caught in her eyes, the lush, artfully painted mouth, those beckoning lips. She possessed some kind of irresistible force that he couldn't name as his thoughts just jumbled.

She was soft and warm and if he was a whimsical man, he might say that she was made for him, for the purpose of sharing the same air, the same space, two halves of a whole. But as a man of science, he realized that it wasn't possible—and Matt did live in the physical world.

"Bedroom?" he whispered.

"Follow me." She started walking toward the nearest closed door, but then backtracked for her purse. Once in the room, Matt pulled her into his arms.

"Before an orgasm, your body becomes increasingly excited," he said. "Breathing, heart rate and blood pressure increase." He kissed her creamy shoulder.

"Check," she murmured.

"The pupils of the eyes dilate, the lips of the mouth darken and tingle."

"Oh yes," she breathed.

His hands framed the sides of her face, holding her still as his mouth took hers, open and hot. His silky tongue thrust and tangled with hers. He deepened the kiss, voracious and hungry, and she answered, sliding her body sensually against his in a rhythm that matched the thrust of his tongue.

Her ripe, full breasts begged for the touch of his fingers, the wet rasp of his tongue, the slow heat of his mouth. "The nipples become erect," he said hoarsely. Her tight buds beckoned his mouth and he lowered his head and put his hot, wet mouth over one rigid nipple and sucked while his other hand fondled her other breast. His cock throbbed and ached.

"Matt," she cried.

"The clitoris swells, becomes hard and exposed, just like my cock swells and hardens for you."

Widening his stance so that his knees bracketed hers, he rolled his hips, grinding his rock-hard sex against the notch between her thighs.

Bridget moaned into his mouth. She dropped her purse and flattened her silky palms against his chest, sliding her hands down his taut abdomen to the waistband of his jeans. Releasing the snap and zipper, she pushed denim and cotton off his hips, freeing him. With a moan of pleasure, he jerked against the exquisite feel of her hand sliding around the base of his shaft, tightening as she stroked him.

He grasped her wrist, knowing that her stimulation would bring him to orgasm way too fast. He'd dreamed about having Bridget come against his mouth. He wasn't going to be denied.

He pressed her back and she folded down onto the bed; he removed the thong.

Reaching over, she grabbed her purse and produced a fistful of condoms. He ripped one open and sheathed himself.

"This is one of my fantasies," he murmured, his gaze coming to a halt at the crux of her thighs. "Having you beneath me so that I could touch you anywhere, do anything."

Lifting a hand, he glided one long finger through the thatch of blond hair and traced the line between her legs, a soft stroke that made her tremble beneath his hand. She moaned and jutted her hips eagerly toward him, and he rewarded her with another brush of his fingertip, just enough to tease her but not appease the hunger he saw in her eyes.

Hooking his fingers beneath her knees, he dragged her toward him. Pushing her knees apart with the palms of his hands, he knelt in front of her. Splaying his hands on her quivering thighs and pushing them farther apart, he gave her no choice but to surrender. He slid his palms upward, and used his thumbs to open her wide, to expose the tender nub of flesh hidden between her legs.

He groaned like a dying man and leaned in closer.

The air in Bridget's lungs felt trapped, and when he used his lush tongue to push delicately inside her, all she could manage was a whimper of sound. He leisurely slipped in and out of her feminine folds, leaving wet, burning trails in his wake.

He found her pulsing clit, and his tongue circled it with wet flicks and slow, suctioning swirls, accelerating her heart rate off the charts. Then his lips closed over her, and he took her eagerly, hotly, greedily, sending her over the jagged edge of orgasm.

She braced herself for the wild ride, and she came with a white-hot burst of passion that made her hips buck and her back arch.

Threading her fingers through Matt's hair, she grasped the strands in her fist and pulled his mouth away. "Matt," she pleaded.

In one fluid, agile movement, he stood, his muscles shifting as he straightened. In another flash, he was on the bed, pulling her lengthwise. He dragged her toward him until her widened thighs were draped over his and her pelvis was tilted up, waiting for him to penetrate her. He eased over her, using his thighs to push hers up higher on his waist. His forearms came to rest next to her face and he shifted his hips, lodging the thick head of his penis against her very core.

Staring into her eyes, he pushed into her an inch, letting her feel the size of him, teasing her with the promise of more. "I can't believe this is happening.

You feel so damn good." His voice deepened to a rough growl.

She touched her fingers to his jaw. "I want to know how you feel."

He plunged into her, strong and deep, impaling her to the hilt with that first unbridled thrust.

Despite being primed for him, she sucked in a startled breath as her inner muscles clamped tight around his shaft. His eyes flared wide in response, giving her a brief glimpse of passion, heat and something else warring in his hot amber depths. Before she could analyze that last emotion, before she could dwell on the initial discomfort of being thoroughly consumed by him, he began to move, his body undulating and grinding against hers as he increased his rhythmic pace.

A low, throaty, on-the-edge moan escaped him, and he crushed his mouth to hers, kissing her with a desperate, fierce passion that caught her off guard. His tongue swept into her mouth, matching the rapid, pistoning stroke of his hips and the slick, penetrating slide of his flesh in hers.

Vibration spread through her from the sensitive spot where they were joined so intimately. She felt thoroughly possessed by him, body and soul, in a way that defied their impersonal bargain and the simplicity of an affair. In a way that aroused feelings that had no business being a part of this temporary relationship.

Pushing those thoughts from her mind, she concentrated on the pleasure he gave her, and how alive he made her body feel. Running her hands down the

slope of his spine, she curved her fingers over his taut
buttocks and locked her legs around his waist to pull
him closer, deeper, and abandoned herself to yet another stunning orgasm.

This time, he was right there with her when she
reached the peak of her climax. Groaning, he broke
their kiss and tossed his head back, his hips driving
hard, his body tightening, straining against hers.

"Bridget." Her name hissed out between his
clenched teeth as his body convulsed with the force
of his release.

When the shudders subsided, Matt lowered himself on top of her and buried his face against her
throat. His ragged breathing was hot and moist
against her skin, his heart racing just as unsteadily
as her own.

A smile drifted across her lips as she trailed her
fingers back up his spine, all the way to the damp,
silky tendrils of hair at the nape of his neck, savoring the delightful feel of him inside her, draped over
her. She'd never felt so utterly satisfied, so sexually,
physically content.

She laughed. "So, my dear scientist, orgasm happens when excitement peaks."

She felt him smile against the skin of her neck.
When he raised his head, his warm eyes regarded her.
"Looks like I proved my hypothesis."

"And how."

For just a moment there was an awkward silence,
but as she stared up into Matt's eyes the awkward-
ness melted away. This was Matt and there was no

need for anything but comfort when she was in his presence.

"Was it worth the wait?" she asked.

He closed his eyes as if he couldn't speak. Finally, he said hoarsely. "I wish I could go back in time and live it all again. You're beautiful when you come. Did you know that?"

She laughed, then groaned—when he shifted inside her, aftershocks of pleasure rippled through her. "What? No, Matt, I don't usually see myself when I'm coming. No mirrors on the ceiling." Bridget draped her legs over the backs of his and smoothed her hands down, slowly mapping the contours of his back.

She moved her hips and he said softly, "Not yet, Bridget, unless I'm too heavy."

"You feel just right," she said.

"I want to savor this moment with you."

Bridget's emotions went crazy, and she closed her eyes and drew a shaky breath, trying to curb the feelings inside her. Opening her eyes, she looked at him, almost afraid to move for fear of doing something to break the spell.

Bracketing her face with his hands, he leaned down and covered her mouth in a drugging kiss. He withdrew from her, taking her with him as he rolled onto his back.

Bridget closed her eyes, her breathing slowed and she drifted off to sleep cradled against Matt.

A HORN BLARED and Bridget jerked awake. She looked at the clock, her sleepy eyes trying to adjust. It read five o'clock. She could hear the sounds of the city surging to life even on a Sunday morning. It was never quiet in New York, taxis honking their horns, traffic continually moving in the street below. But she'd gotten used to the noise and bustle of the city. It even lulled her to sleep at night.

She rolled away from the warmth of Matt, suddenly wide awake. His face was peaceful in sleep and so handsome she had to catch her breath.

She sighed deeply. The man knew what he was doing, that was for sure. Her whole body tingled at the thought of what he'd done to her with his sexy, deep voice and his clever hands and mouth. He'd been bold and dominant, yet so generous with her pleasure, and she'd been greedy and utterly shameless. Even though her curiosity had been satisfied, she wanted more of Matt.

Then she remembered his job offer. She hadn't had a moment to let that information seep in last night once Matt had put his hands on her. But now she realized that she had a job and could likely pay off some of her debts. Breathing a sigh of relief, she slipped from the bed and let Matt sleep.

One small niggling doubt reared its ugly head. She didn't know the first thing about starting up a business or about marketing. She expected that she was about to learn.

Going out into the living room, she picked up Matt's discarded T-shirt and slipped it over her head. The smell of him enveloped her and she breathed in his scent. Reaching down into her tote, she pulled out a sketch pad.

She worked steadily on her drawing, losing track of time as the sky outside the window brightened and the traffic noise increased.

"Hey?"

Bridget looked up from her sketch pad to see Matt wearing only his new soft, faded jeans that were slung low on his hips, nothing else. His dark hair was a disheveled, enticing mess. He looked so sinfully sexy he literally took her breath away and made her ache in a way no man had ever managed with just a searing sloe-eyed glance from those devastating amber eyes of his.

The dreams and fantasies of Matt that she'd spun over the past week paled in comparison to the real thing.

With deceptive laziness, he folded his arms across his broad, bare chest and leaned casually against the door frame, his entire demeanor vibrating with a playful edge.

How many more pearls was she going to discover? The exploration excited her.

"Hey, yourself."

"If you're going to get up this early, you should have at least brewed some coffee," he said, his tone light and flirtatious.

She rolled her eyes at him, her lips curving. "Sleep with a guy and he expects you to wait on him hand and foot. Brew your own coffee, mister."

His lips curved even deeper as he slowly shook his head. "I'm a guest," he said, pushing off the door frame and walking toward the couch. "Guests don't make coffee."

He stopped close to her, his shin almost touching her bare thigh. "You're not a guest," she said. "You're just the guy I'm banging."

He went for her waist and as soon as his fingers dug in, Bridget squirmed to get free. "No, Matt. Stop tickling me, you animal."

"You're the one who's dishing out the cruel and inhumane punishment."

"All right. Uncle! Uncle!" she sputtered. "I'll make you some coffee."

He let her go and sat down next to her on the couch. Bridget got up and went into the kitchen and filled her glass carafe with cold water.

"You look much better in that T-shirt than I did, but it's a little short."

She gave him a sultry look over her shoulder. "I know."

"*Raspberry* is your color, though. It compliments your nice backside."

She opened the cover and reached for the filter as the T-shirt rode higher on her hips.

"Bridget, you are so beautiful."

She meant to say teasingly, *I bet you say that to all the girls in short T-shirts,* but when her eyes met his, the bright flare of hunger in his stare and the dark, edgy beauty of his aroused expression stole her breath. But there was more there, a wealth of emotion, a scary connection. That connection jumbled everything inside her. She fumbled the filter and it dropped to the floor. As she bent to pick it up, she heard a rustle of paper.

"What's this?"

She straightened and saw that he held her sketch pad. "My attempt to draw a design for your fabric." She inserted a filter and filled the basket with ground coffee.

"This is…um…very sexy, Bridget. You're really talented."

She shrugged, feeling uncomfortable with his genuine praise. He started to flip through the other drawings and Bridget turned on the coffeepot to start it brewing.

She walked back to the couch and sat down next to him.

"When did you do these?"

"I bring the pad with me to all my shoots. I sometimes have to wait hours before I'm needed. Doodling passes the time."

"It's more than doodling. Did you make any of these?"

"I used to make a lot of my own clothes. But when the modeling took off it pulled me in different directions, and I didn't have time. But I can't seem to stop drawing the images in my head. Those never go away."

"Maybe your heart is trying to tell you something." He flipped back to the drawing she'd worked on early this morning.

She shrugged, her tone dismissive. "It's just for fun. Do you like it?"

He set the sketch pad aside. This time when he grabbed her waist, he pulled her across his lap. "I'd like to see you in it."

Her hand shot out, splaying against his hard, virile chest. Without another word, she slid her flattened hand up his taut chest, along his shoulder, and curled her fingers along his nape. Silently, she pulled his mouth close to hers and said in a husky tone, "You're the boss, so if you say I have to model it for you, I won't be able to resist." Her mouth brushed his and his hips surged up, his erection hot and firm against her.

"There are some perks to the job, then."

"Oh yeah," she said softly, moving her hips against his hard heat. "There are some great perks."

BRIDGET CUT the pink thread, Matt's fabric soft and pliant beneath her fingers. Back at her aunt Ida's house it was early Tuesday morning, the sun just kissing the horizon. Matt had driven his father's car back to Cambridge and dropped Bridget at her aunt's on Sunday. Before he'd gone home, he gave her the name of his manufacturer and she'd already called the business office yesterday to order more bolts of the fabric and sign the contract they'd sent her.

The moment she'd stepped in the house, her cell phone rang and her agent said that she'd need her in New York for a go-see that afternoon, so she'd boarded a plane an hour later, frustrated that she couldn't start on making the sexy outfit she'd drawn at her loft.

When she got back Monday night, Matt wasn't at home, so she'd started looking for her aunt's old sewing machine. Then there was a flurry of activity, refining her drawing, making a pattern, rolling out

Matt's fabric and, with a deep breath, cutting the cloth. That's all she'd had time for yesterday. Unable to lie still, sheer mental energy drove her early from her bed and she'd started to sew the T-shirt together.

But she had to admit that her restless slumber had a lot to do with Matt. Sensual memories and tantalizing images of him transferred into provocative dreams. Even now with the silky material between her fingers, her concentration vital to keep the stitches straight, she found her focus fragmenting.

Just the memory of him made her heart flutter and she had to admit that her heart hadn't fluttered in a long time. Even surrounded by gorgeous male models. She couldn't imagine any other man's eyes being as warm and compassionate as Matt's.

She couldn't get him off her mind for even a minute. His lean, handsome face, all planes and angles. The sexy devastating way he grinned.

There was that stupid flutter again.

And his hard, taut body was now the focus of feverish erotic dreams in the privacy of her bed. He had grown so tall and muscular, the honed lean body of a boxer. After what they'd shared, she wanted to explore every inch of his body. Delve deep into those endless pools of his eyes and drown.

She couldn't afford to lose her head over him, although a little one-on-one body contact couldn't hurt. Could it?

Matt wasn't in her plan of action. The visit with Aunt Ida was only a stopgap on the path to her getting back into the fashion biz.

Except he was damn distracting. Even now she struggled with the image of the boy he'd been and the man he'd become. As a child, he'd always been quiet and shy whenever he'd eaten dinner at Aunt Ida's, a solid presence when he'd helped her with her homework, studious and diligent. So very smart.

Smarter than she, that was for sure. But Bridget hadn't worried much about that in school. She knew where her strengths were—her beauty and ability to talk her way into just about anything she put her mind to.

So, when she'd been crowned Miss National, she'd taken the modeling lessons prize instead of the scholarship to a university of her choice and had never looked back. Did she now have regrets about giving up the scholarship and a more academic path? Maybe.

She pulled the completed T-shirt from the machine and turned it inside out. She picked up the already threaded needle and a large flower appliqué she'd made yesterday, dying it a darker shade of pink.

She'd almost completed attaching all the flower appliqués when there was a knock on her door and her aunt stuck her head in. "Hey there." Her aunt walked farther into the room. "You've been busy, honey. I thought this was a visit." She walked over to Bridget and picked up something from her worktable. "What's this?"

"A pattern. Goes with this." Bridget showed her aunt the exquisite top she was working on to match the pattern of the boy briefs her aunt held in her hands.

"Are you making the clothes now instead of wearing them?"

"No." She smiled. "I'm helping Matt out with a business venture. He invented this cloth."

"Matt's a smart boy, but spends much too much time alone. I can see it didn't take you long to get acquainted again."

"The kiss goodbye Sunday when he dropped me off. You saw that?"

"There isn't much these wise eyes miss, honey."

"Matt and I have a special connection. We just took the next step."

"He's mighty fine."

"Aunt Ida."

"There might be snow on the roof, but there's still a fire in the hearth. Matt's gorgeous—I noticed."

"You're something, Aunt Ida." Bridget finished the flower and held the shirt up by the shoulders to look at it.

Her aunt took the garment out of her hands. "This is beautiful. You designed this?"

"Yeah. I wanted to see how the fabric moved and how comfortable it is to sleep in."

"Maybe you *ought* to think about making the clothes."

"No, it's just doodling. My strength is in modeling them. I'm real good at posing."

"That's true, but I do really like this. It speaks to the female voice inside you that likes pretty things." Her aunt handed her back the garment. "I'd better get myself to the hospital."

"Have a good day. And Aunt Ida…thanks so very much…for everything."

Her aunt smoothed her hand over Bridget's head. "You know that you always have a place here with me, honey, but you should really call your mother."

Bridget met her aunt's eyes and there was something there that made Bridget wonder how much she was ever able to put over on her aunt. It was never spoken out loud, but her aunt always understood what Bridget needed when she was a child. Perhaps she understood more what she might need as an adult.

Still, Bridget couldn't seem to make herself speak and when her cell phone rang, the moment was lost. Bridget nodded and snatched it up, hoping it was Leslie on the other end with a contract from Maggie Winterbourne. "Hello," she said.

"Miss Cole?"

"Yes."

"I'm a reporter with *On* magazine and I got your number from your agent. I was hoping to interview you for a piece we're doing on former Miss National winners."

"A where-are-they-now kind of piece?"

"Exactly."

Bridget cringed at the thought of describing where she was now, but then immediately brightened. She could get Matt some much-needed publicity if she glossed over her job woes and played up her CEO status while mentioning Matt's great fabric. This gig with Matt was temporary, not her modeling career, but she was sure she could put some kind of spin on it. "That would be great."

"Is now a good time?"

"Now would be fine," she said.

On magazine had a huge readership. It couldn't hurt to talk to the guy. She wouldn't have to reveal too many facts at this point. This was most likely a fluff piece.

She, after all, was the one who was supposed to make the decisions. She was the CEO.

And she knew she had Matt's trust.

And that meant a lot to her.

After she disconnected the call from the reporter, her cell rang again. "Bridget, I got you a job, but it's in Puerto Rico. Can you grab a flight from Logan?"

Bridget looked down at the fabric in her hands. It would have to wait. "Yes, what time?"

Leslie gave her the flight details.

"How long?"

"A week. Did you get the call from *On?*"

"Yes, just now."

"Good. That may generate some interest. Talk to you later."

"Thanks, Leslie."

Bridget bustled around her room, packing what she needed. She picked up her cell phone and called Matt. His sleepy voice answered. She told him what was happening and promised to see him when she got back.

MATT DESCENDED THE STAIRS with his students' graded papers and his suit jacket. He put the stack of exams in his briefcase and clicked the top closed.

Smoothing out the jacket, he hung it on the back of one of his kitchen chairs.

Bridget had been gone a week and he was hoping she'd be back today.

There was a knock on the door and he looked down at his watch in surprise. He didn't expect his lunch party for another hour.

He pulled open the door to discover that dessert had arrived ahead of schedule. Bridget looked good enough to eat in the hot pink bathing suit cover-up she'd been wearing last week on Saturday.

"Welcome back. Are you going for a swim?" he asked, perplexed as to why she had the edges of the cover-up clasped in her closed fist and a magazine and newspaper in the other.

"No. I wanted to show you this. I forgot to tell you about it before I left."

He took the magazine she thrust out to him. Her picture was on the cover with a headline that read Miss National. Where Are They Now?

"On?" Matt felt a sudden uneasy feeling crawl across his skin. "That's a national magazine."

"I thought it would be good publicity for your fabric and your business. Was I wrong?"

He reassured himself that she was the public face on the company and he had nothing to worry about. He could stay anonymous. "Yes, of course, it is good publicity."

"I didn't expect this, though."

She handed him the newspaper folded open to the fashion section. He read the headline of the short article.

New CEO Announces Revolutionary Fabric—
Almostaked™. Matt's unbelieving eyes scanned the
first paragraph of the article.

Bridget Cole isn't your ordinary CEO. But
that's no surprise. She's a former Miss National. For years, pageants like Miss National
have been vehicles with which women pursued
career-related aspirations. Cole knew wearing
the crown would bring instant fame, trips
across the country and invitations to premiere
social events. She knew winning meant giving
speeches to thousands of people across the nation—including heads of major corporations—
and raising awareness for charities. With all
that training and her ten years as a fashion
model, this position is tailor-made for this former winner. The company, Almost Naked, Inc.,
will focus on marketing a new lingerie fabric
that will revolutionize the women's apparel
market. Cole states that, "This fabric is softer
than silk, much more comfortable, washable
and it breathes just like cotton." Imagine that,
ladies, comfortable lingerie. She's sure to take
the fabric world by storm.

"The newspaper must have picked up on the *On*
article. Matt, say something."

"Almost Naked, Inc."

"Yeah. I thought it was eye-catching."

"That it is. And you named the fabric."

"Sure. I said that's what it feels like against my skin."

"Do you have any more surprises up your sleeves?"

She stepped inside and he closed the door. When he turned around she pulled open the cover-up and let it fall. "Just this."

She knew how to make a dramatic statement. Her tousled blond hair lay loose around her silk-clad shoulders. Slumberous blue eyes focused on him and her lips formed a slow, sensual smile that made him feel sucker punched.

Matt lost all train of thought. Everything flew right out of his head as if it had never existed. He just took her in with one big, greedy gulp, unable to get enough. He knew he was supposed to be doing something, but her beauty pulled him in like a vortex, potent and exhilarating and wholly irresistible.

Bridget wore a formfitting pale pink diaphanous T-shirt, decorated with darker pink flowers. The see-through material left absolutely nothing to the imagination. The sight of her full, rounded breasts pressed tight against the fabric made his fingers itch to touch her. One enticing nipple formed the center of one flower. He ached to close his mouth over it and taste her sweet nectar. His eyes followed the line of her body down past her flat stomach to her hips where she wore a matching pair of boy briefs in the same sexy color.

While his eyes lingered and brazenly raked over her body, she watched him, her own eyes roving hungrily over his face.

He wanted her as he had never hungered for anything before, even knowledge. That rocked him back on his heels and his gut tightened. She was pure, unadulterated pleasure.

His eyes traveled over her face again and down her elegant neck to her breasts.

She would be a high-maintenance woman with her unending well of energy. She would take his attention and invade his privacy right down to his soul. Somehow, right now, he couldn't care.

"What do you think?"

"I'll let you know as soon as I finish swallowing my tongue."

"You like it."

"You have to ask? Isn't the stunned expression on my face enough?"

"I need you to say it, Matt. Will it do?"

His thoughts about doing had nothing at all to do with the fabric. "Bridget, it's beautiful, sexy, mind-numbing. Blood is surging to the naughty parts of my body."

She breathed a sigh of relief. "Good. I'm going to sleep in it tonight, get familiar with the fabric, but it feels amazing against my skin. I can't believe this fabric was a *mistake*. When normal people make a mistake, it usually turns out bad."

"Oh, this is bad," he said, closing the short distance between them. "Very, very bad."

He took her mouth in a fast, hard kiss, pushing his hips tight up against hers and rushing them both beyond control. She pushed back just as fiercely.

He drew one hand slowly down between them, his hips still joined to hers…and their gazes locked on each other.

Neither said a word as he brushed his thumb over that tantalizing nipple. "I don't know what's softer, the fabric or your delectable body."

His eyes caressed her face as he gently pinched her nipple between his fingers. She groaned softly, her hands pushing his jacket off his shoulders, unbuckling his pants.

Her clothes disappeared and his pants ended up around his ankles as he pushed her back onto the couch. Bracing his forearms on either side of her shoulders and settling himself between her legs, he dropped his head against her neck and groaned as he impaled her to the hilt. Her back bowed as he began to move in earnest, his strokes growing faster, harder, stronger….

When he opened his eyes, her face was inches away from his as he continued to thrust into her, her blue eyes so intense they burned straight to his soul, and he knew in that moment that he'd never be the same again.

He called out her name as their bodies convulsed, his orgasm slamming into him with a physically powerful force, mingling with the need to be close to this woman.

Long minutes later, he released her, sitting back to give her some breathing room. Bridget didn't move.

"You were going somewhere, weren't you? I messed you all up. I know I rushed over here unannounced, but I was so excited about getting on the cover of *On,* the newspaper article and how the outfit turned out."

Matt didn't answer as the knock on his front door interrupted their conversation and brought memory flooding back. He was having lunch with two colleagues from MIT.

He scrambled off the couch, fumbling for his clothes. They couldn't see Bridget here. A lot of people read *On.* It was possible they could see her and put him and Almost Naked together.

"Get dressed," he said a little more sharply than he'd meant to in light of what they'd just shared.

"What's wrong?"

"My secret is in jeopardy."

5

THAT WAS THE FASTEST she'd ever seen a human being dress. And she should know. She'd been in plenty of runway shows. He'd grabbed up the sexy outfit that he'd just gotten her out of and rushed her into the downstairs bathroom.

Dying of curiosity, she peered out of the slightly ajar door. Matt and a woman were standing close to the couch and there was another person just out of her eyesight. It was then she saw her cover-up. Oh, damn.

With a sly look on her face, the woman picked it up. She said, "Matt, do you have a new girlfriend you didn't tell me about?"

Matt cleared his throat. "Ah, no, it belongs to the woman next door."

For one irrational second, she felt stung that Matt couldn't claim her, in any way, not as a friend and surely, not as a girlfriend.

"Okay," the sly woman said. "She has really good taste."

So Matt knew this woman well. Irritation sent heat rushing through Bridget's body and to her face. Her irrational anger was weird and uncharacteristic.

Any woman who had the good fashion taste to covet a stylish piece of clothing was worth getting to know.

Exploding out of Matt's bathroom dressed in her provocative outfit would be sheer lunacy, she knew, thus she continued to watch, curbing the overwhelming urge.

She was peeved. He didn't want her to meet his friends. He couldn't even take a moment to kiss her. That was a man for you.

She would have made a great impression on his friends. Even after being fully ravished on his couch, Bridget knew how to present herself. She sighed. Of course, she knew it was because of his worry about being exposed, but she still felt miffed. Only a few minutes ago, she'd been entwined around his naked body.

As soon as they exited the house, Bridget made her way to the couch and snatched her cover-up. Donning it, she walked to the window and peered out, getting an unobstructed look at the woman. Matt was talking to her in the driveway as they made their way down to a waiting car at the curb. She was impeccably dressed in a Donna Karan lime-green blazer and black pants. Her dark hair fell in a stylish cut that had to have cost at least two hundred bucks. She was wearing black Kenneth Cole croc pumps, taking long strides to keep up with Matt.

While Bridget watched, Matt's companion slipped her arm through his and Bridget narrowed her eyes. Although the woman had great taste in clothes and men, Bridget wanted to rip her apart for even touching Matt. He was hers.

Whoa. He wasn't hers. He couldn't be hers. She wouldn't be staying around Cambridge long enough to build any kind of lasting relationship. It was just a matter of time before she went back to her life in New York. She turned away, unable to look at them any longer. She had to wonder who the woman was, since Matt had rushed out before he'd given her an explanation. She suspected that she must be a colleague.

Bridget was sure the woman had plenty to talk to Matt about. The intricacies of chemistry and whatever else it took to invent fabrics was much more interesting than Bridget's little sexy outfit. She felt stupid and she so hated feeling stupid. She was pretty sure that Miss Donna Karan was much more stimulating intellectually than Bridget could ever hope to be.

She went to the front door, planning to slip out and lock it behind her, but realized too late that Matt and his lunch party were still at the curb. The woman turned her head just as Bridget stepped out. Feeling like a deer caught in the headlights of an onrushing car, Bridget froze. The woman got a good look at her goofy oh-no-I've-been-caught face before Bridget jumped back and quickly shut the door.

Hopefully Matt was wrong and the woman wouldn't recognize her from the article in the paper or the *On* piece. Did brainy types even read *On?*

Yet a nagging doubt lingered. The woman was so put together and knew her fashion. Maybe she had it all—brains, beauty and taste.

Bridget sneaked over to the window, standing far enough to the side to be able to make sure that the car had pulled away from the curb. Feeling like a fool, she walked back to the front door and left Matt's house.

It was time to stop fooling around. She had a business to build. She hoped after Matt finished with lunch, she'd still have a job.

HOURS LATER, Bridget's gut squeezed into a tight fist and she was pretty certain she was going to throw up. She'd decided it was time to find out exactly how to start a business, and she'd consulted the Internet. The sheer volume of material made her head swim. What the heck had she gotten herself into? How was she going to keep her creative flow if she had to worry about marketing and business plans and, God forbid, a mission statement? She certainly couldn't go to Matt and quit. She'd barely begun, and she really needed the job. She sat back in her aunt's comfy office chair and stared at the computer.

Taking a deep breath, she picked up the phone and dialed.

"Carlyle Business Services."

"May I speak with Naomi Carlyle," Bridget said with just a tad of panic in her voice. *Keep your cool,* she told herself sternly.

When Naomi came on the line Bridget said, "I'll pay you a huge consulting fee if you come to Cambridge and help me. I'll pick up the expenses, too."

"Bridget?"

"Yes."

"What's wrong?"

"I got a job and I need your help."

"What have you gotten yourself into?"

Bridget could picture Naomi in her posh office, sitting in her high-backed leather chair with a breathtaking view of the city. All she had to offer the girl was a messy bedroom and a small office with a view of the hot tub in the backyard. A far cry from big business.

Bridget ran her free hand through her hair, feeling that familiar wad of dread in her stomach that appeared whenever she had to admit that she couldn't handle something. She'd spent so much time in her life protecting her image that it terrified her to reveal any weakness to anyone. But she needed Naomi's help. "I've gotten myself into a situation that is a little over my head."

There was silence for a moment as if Naomi was shocked at Bridget's confession, a step back in a relationship that had been teetering on full-blown friendship.

"What kind of situation?" Naomi asked, her voice sharpening.

"I'm the new CEO of a company marketing a revolutionary new fabric."

"Really?" Naomi said with admiration. "How did you manage that?"

"It's too much to go into right now. I'll explain it to you later."

"What exactly is the problem, then?" Naomi asked, her voice softening. The confidence that Naomi projected always made Bridget feel at ease and gave her hope that her almost friend would take what Bridget was offering.

"The fabric," Bridget said.

"Marketing the fabric?"

Feeling antsy, Bridget got up and walked to the back door. Stepping outside, she paced the length of her aunt's patio, her chest tightening up on her. "It's a little more involved than that. I need to incorporate."

"Oh," Naomi said in total understanding. "Have you filed the paperwork?"

"Paperwork? Ah, no."

"Do you have a business plan?"

Bridget gritted her teeth. "No again."

"Marketing plan?"

Bridget sighed, and looked down at the sparkling aquamarine of the pool. She thought of just leaning over and soaking her head. Instead, she kicked off her shoes and sat down at the edge of the pool. Dipping her feet into the cool water, she said wryly, "Three strikes."

"Okay." Naomi's voice was full of reassurance. "What about the fabric? Do you have a manufacturer?"

"Yes! Matt gave me the name of the business he used. I've already put in a large order and signed a contract. I did something right."

"Ah, Bridget, do you have buyers?"

"No, not yet."

Bridget's enthusiasm was short-lived. There was once again silence at the end of the line. "I hate to break the news to you, but the International Fashion Fabric Exhibition was three months ago."

The ominous tone of Naomi's voice sent a shiver down Bridget's spine. She pulled her feet out of the water and started pacing again. "What does that mean?"

"Well, buyers from all over the world go there specifically to purchase for spring-summer of the following year. I work for a few designers and I know some of the buyers came back with some sensational fabrics."

Exhausted, Bridget collapsed into a wicker chaise and leaned her head back, closing her eyes. "So there's no way to sell without going to an exhibition?"

"Yes, of course there is, but it's going to take a lot more work."

"How much time do you think?"

"You'll have to contact each buyer, whereas at an exhibition they are readily available."

"So, I have tons of fabric and no buyers. I didn't think this would be a problem. Matt's going to kill me."

"So, an all-expenses-paid trip to Cambridge. I charge a hefty consulting rate."

"No problem."

"How can I turn that down? Sounds like a great challenge. I've always wanted to start at the ground floor of a business," Naomi said in a teasing voice.

Bridget silently thanked her for the attempt at levity. But, unfortunately, Bridget couldn't find anything amusing about her predicament. "Thank you so much, Naomi, I'm desperate."

"A little tip for you, girlfriend. In the marketing world, don't let anyone know that you're desperate."

NAOMI'S WORDS CAME BACK TO HER when Bridget heard Matt's voice down in her aunt's foyer. It was also true in the relationship department. She'd spent too much time thinking about Matt and her renewed connection with him. She lamented the years she'd lost touch with him, sorry that she hadn't kept up with his friendship. It was the warmth in those damn arresting eyes that had drawn her back into that need she'd had as a child.

She'd wanted Matt's approval. He gave it freely without any strings attached. Her mother had pushed her so hard when she'd been a little girl, it was all Bridget knew. She had to be the best, she had to succeed. It was Matt who had been the calm water in the eye of the hurricane that was her mother. She really thought she might have turned out a cold, shallow, selfish bitch if it hadn't been for Matt.

So, it had been easy to slip back into confiding in him, rebuilding that personal and emotional relationship she'd had with him, adding the more complicated physical one. But Bridget wondered what Matt thought about it all. Perhaps he found her ambitions and her jockeying to get ahead pathetic. It served her right. Matt had never coveted fame and fortune, but it had dropped into his lap. It seemed poetic justice that it had eluded her.

She had been just about ready to jump in the shower. It was Thursday morning, two days since she'd talked to Naomi, and her new business manager would arrive at Logan at one o'clock today. That was only three hours from now and Bridget just didn't have the time, or the right frame of mind to deal with Matt.

Plus it had been two days since she'd seen him. *Two days!*

It wasn't as if she'd expected flowers and candy or for Matt to declare his undying love, but some contact would have been nice. She'd even gone over to his house and knocked, then banged, but he hadn't answered, though his car was in the driveway.

She had thought about climbing the dangerous trellis just to be able to tell him off, but in a lucid break in her snit she decided it wasn't worth a broken neck.

She'd also had the thought that perhaps if she had climbed the trellis that Donna Karan woman would be in his bed. Maybe he had some kind of relationship with her for all Bridget knew. She hadn't seen Matt since she was sixteen. Twelve years was a lot of time.

So she was feeling especially cranky and out of sorts when she heard his voice. He continued to talk to her aunt, the sound of his sexy voice drifting up to her room. She closed her eyes.

"Bridget?" His voice so close made her jump. She whirled around to find him standing in her doorway. Why did he have to look so disarmingly cute, so sinfully sexy with his spiky black hair and upturned eyes?

"Look, you have every right to be mad. I rushed out on you after we had sex and I've ignored you the past few days. I'm sorry."

Her jaw dropped open and she stared at him. He'd

come right to the point. No cute sashaying, no trying to wheedle back into her good graces, none of that juvenile guy stuff she hated.

He waved his hand as he came into the room and closed the door. "I don't believe in subterfuge, Bridget. It only gets in the way." He stopped in front of her. "The trouble is I was working and I get crazy when I work. Sometimes a couple of days pass before I realize it."

Jeez, he was killing her. She could feel the heat of his body, could smell his clean, masculine scent.

He stepped closer, wreaking havoc with her hormones and common sense.

"You kept bothering me, though."

Bridget stiffened. "I knocked on your door only once."

He smiled as if her indignation was a great source of amusement to him. "I wasn't talking about you literally bothering me. I was talking about how I couldn't stop thinking about doing this."

He lowered his head, the light in his eyes dancing with need, and the moment their lips touched she gave herself over to the exquisite feel of his mouth on hers, the rich, addictive taste of him on her tongue, and the promise of pleasures untold as he deepened the kiss even more.

A shameless moan rumbled up from her throat, and she wrapped her arms around his neck and arched against him. She felt his hard, thick erection at the crux of her thighs, reveled in it and grew wet with wanting.

He wrapped his hands around her waist and lifted her onto the bed. She watched the play of pleasure across his face as his hands slid up her sides. When he reached her breasts, his palms kneaded the slopes and his thumbs lazily circled her hypersensitive nipples.

She threaded her fingers through the soft strands of his hair and groaned as his lips burned a path across her jaw, along her throat. "Matt."

For a moment they just lay there, breathing heavily together, their chests rising and falling. Finally, Matt lifted up on one elbow and stared down into her eyes.

"You doing okay?" he asked, and gently brushed a strand of hair off her cheek with his fingers.

The warmth and compassion in his touch lingered, wrapping intimately around her heart, urging her to divulge her personal thoughts. She bit her lip. "What happened to us, Matt?"

"What do you mean?"

"Why didn't we stay friends?"

"I don't know. We drifted apart. You had the pageants and after the stunt you pulled with the unauthorized party, your mother refused to let you visit your aunt."

"I have this feeling my mother wants to keep us apart. Did you see how she reacted at Aunt Ida's birthday party?"

The genuine caring reflected in his striking eyes was nearly her undoing. "I told you she didn't like me."

"But why?"

"I think she sees me as a threat, Bridget. Then, she didn't want you distracted from her obsession to see you crowned Miss National. Now, she simply doesn't want you distracted. Period."

"I wanted that crown, too, Matt. You talk like I was her beauty-queen slave." Her voice trembled, another show of emotion that slipped past her barriers.

"You've been entered in pageants since you were six, Bridget. How would you know what you wanted?"

"I know what I want. Don't try to confuse me. We're in a business venture together and we're in bed together."

"It's more than sexual."

"I know. I didn't even realize how lonely I was until I saw you again."

"It breaks my heart to think that you have been lonely, sweetheart."

"You're so sweet, Matt."

"Not that sweet. I did ignore you for two days."

"Yes, you did. But I understand why. You'll have to make it up to me for leaving so quickly after making love to me. Also, I need to tell you that the woman you were with saw me."

"She did? She didn't mention it."

"So who is that woman?"

"She's my wife."

Bridget jerked, her hands coming up to push against Matt's chest. She felt satisfied at the thud he made when he hit the floor.

Leaning over the edge of the bed, she glared at him. "What the hell did you say?"

6

MATT KNEW HE WAS IN DEEP trouble the moment he saw those stormy blue eyes and realized what he'd said. It was easy to rectify with a simple explanation. Although he'd been in trouble with a woman before, it hadn't scared him.

Bridget Cole, on the other hand, terrified him.

He reached up and grabbed at her before she could scoot away. With a soft exclamation, Bridget slipped off the bed onto his chest.

"A slip of the tongue. She's my *ex*-wife," he said.

She stared at him a moment and the enormous relief he saw in her eyes made something coil tight and dangerous in his gut.

"Some people would think that was a Freudian slip and you really wanted to be married to her again."

"Believe me. It was an honest mistake. Emily and I don't work as a married couple. I'm much more interested in discussing how lovely your eyes are, or how sweet you taste."

"Wait just a second, Mr. Smoothie. Not so fast. Why didn't you tell me you were married?"

"It's a part of my life that's over. We didn't even make it to our first anniversary. I've gotten past it. She works at MIT, too."

"I don't understand why you didn't think it was important enough to tell me…. Here I was going crazy thinking this woman—" She broke off, snapped her mouth shut.

Matt's heart felt as if it slipped…and settled, right into the place it had always belonged. "Part of my problem with the marriage was that she never really understood me. We never shared the kind of closeness I've only experienced with one woman in my life."

"Who is that?" Bridget demanded, ready to get up off him.

He laughed and her eyes narrowed. "You."

Her eyes softened, and then flared to blue flame. "Oh. Good." She lowered her head and took his mouth. She tasted raw, undiluted. Real. He wove his fingers through her hair. It felt like a silk waterfall. Erotic, tactile…cool to the touch.

He brushed his mouth against her lips, then sucked her lower lip into his mouth. He was unable to resist, her mouth was so full and perfect, taunting him. "You taste delicious and forbidden," he told her. "Too delectable to pass up."

She laughed against his mouth. "I have no protest to being eaten by you, Matt."

"Don't tempt me."

He grinned when she rolled her eyes. "I think I like tempting you. I like watching your eyes go all glassy. When you look at me, it gives me chills."

"If you're trying to make me crazy, you're succeeding," Matt said, cupping her face. "So stop it."

"Fine, you win."

"Good. I like to win."

That brought more laughter bubbling out of her and he decided that he liked the deep rich tone. He smiled against her lips as she crushed her mouth to his. The laughter quickly faded, however, as she slid her tongue into his mouth. He groaned and accepted the invasion willingly. She knew how to kiss a man.

He was also startled to discover that her body aligned so perfectly with his. Knee-to-knee, hip-to-hip…and, most startlingly, pelvis-to-pelvis. A novel experience for his height.

She wove her fingers through his hair, making his skin tingle as her nails raked his scalp, then angled her head and took the kiss deeper. He'd thought to taunt her a little, tease her a little and brighten up both of their days with a little harmless flirtation, just for the sheer fun of it.

But the hunger she'd ignited in him had been something he hadn't counted on. She made him feel downright…barbaric.

He raised his hips off the floor, seeking harder contact with her. She gasped at the feel of him, so perfectly fitted to her and pushed back.

His lips drifted down her chin, which she tilted, giving him all the access he could want to the soft skin of her throat. "I don't have the words to tell you how much I want you."

"No words. Speechless."

He reared up, his breathing harsh and labored. He nuzzled his open mouth across her sleek skin, the taste of her overwhelming him as he moved his tongue over her breast.

She arched, a tightly strung bow, to his mouth.

Her small hands curled around his neck, brushing his throat, and he shivered.

He was lost to everything except the taste of her, the supple sleek feel of her skin against his lips, and in his ears the only sound was the rhythm of her heart beating with his.

Everywhere he felt her light touch against him, an awareness of her beyond anything he had ever experienced or ever imagined. And he'd imagined a lot with Bridget. Slanting her to him, one palm cupping her hip, the other still tangled in the unruly mass of her hair, he tasted her again and again. She had shaken his foundation down to the core and he knew. He knew that this couldn't last, that she'd go jet-setting off as soon as she was back on her feet, but he couldn't regret what they had done together.

What he had fretted about had come to fruition. She was distracting him, drawing him away from his work. She was burrowing under his skin and he didn't know how he was going to handle it later.

Then he glanced at her face and thought he might drown in those eyes of hers. So bold, so honest...so full of want. For him.

He watched her intently as he rolled her nipple between his fingers. Her pupils dilated, and her lips parted in a silent gasp. But her eyes remained open, and on him. Almost like a challenge. One he desperately wanted to be up to.

"Touching you. It's such a damn turn-on for me."

"Everything about you turns me on, Matt."

"Mmm, everything, huh?"

"Yes," she said, her hands sliding hard over his biceps as she cupped his face, her thumbs rubbing at the skin of his cheeks. "The fire that is in your eyes right now. The color of them, the exotic slant, and your full mouth." She leaned forward and kissed him gently, then changed the angle of her head and captured his mouth again.

The sudden sound of the door opening and closing made them both stiffen.

"My aunt?"

"I don't think so...."

"Bridget?" A female voice called.

"Ohmigod! It's my mother."

Matt heard heavy footsteps on the stairs. "She's coming right now."

Bridget was off him in a flash. "Matt, hide in the bathroom." When he began to move, she hissed. "Never mind. It's too late. Scoot under the bed."

"Bridget, I'm a grown man. You're a grown woman."

"Please, Matt. It's too embarrassing."

Matt had no more time to argue with her about the ridiculousness of a full-grown man hiding under the bed. It wasn't as if they were sixteen years old for crying out loud. But to spare Bridget the comments he was sure her mother would make about having sex in the middle of the day, he slid under the bed just as Mrs. Cole opened Bridget's door.

It was a tight, uncomfortable fit, his chest wedged against the hard metal of the box spring. Dust tickled his nose and he turned his head and brought his hand up to rub it so he wouldn't sneeze. Talk about humiliation.

"There you are, you naughty girl," Bridget's mother said.

"Mom. What a surprise." Bridget's feet moved from her position beside the bed to the footboard. He could only envision her taking her mother's arm and moving her back toward the door as their feet met and moved away from the bed.

"I bet it is. You've been in Cambridge all this time and didn't call me for lunch?"

He rubbed his nose again as their feet stopped just shy of the door.

"I'm sorry about that, but how about I give you a call next week? I really can't talk now, Mom. I've got an appointment."

"You know I've been waiting impatiently for news about your photo shoot in Puerto Rico. Let's sit down and you can fill me in."

Matt almost groaned at the thought of having to hide up here through girl talk.

"I can't, Mom. As I just mentioned, I've got an appointment."

"What appointment?"

"I've got to get to the airport and pick up a friend. Her plane is due in an hour."

"Friend? What friend?"

"Naomi from New York City."

"Your CPA?"

"Yes, she's consulting for me."

"On what?"

"A business venture I'm working on with Matt."

"What? Has he done this? Convinced you to give up such a wonderful modeling career? Do you know what I sacrificed for you?"

"As you've told me countless times. Look. I really don't have time...."

"Of all the ungrateful... What is going on, Bridget?"

"I told you. I'm working for Matt."

"What does that loser next door have to do with your fashion career?"

"He's not a loser, Mom. He's got his Ph.D., for Pete's sake. He's teaching at MIT."

"What exactly are you doing for him?"

"Look, we can meet later to talk about this. I really have to go get in the shower." Matt sighed in relief as their feet started to move again.

"I'm not going anywhere until I've heard your answer," her mother replied.

"I've accepted a position to market a new fabric for him. Okay, Mother. Now let me walk you down to the front door."

"What? What do you know about starting a venture or marketing? Are you out of your mind? Is this what you're doing? Drawing and making clothes?"

Matt heard a rustle of paper.

"Mother, calm down. It's just temporary."

"Calm down. I knew that boy was trouble even back then. Always filling your head full of nonsense. As if all the beauty pageants were a waste of your time. I never saw such a rude—"

"He didn't fill my head full of nonsense. He helped me with my math and taught me all about astronomy."

"He was a troublemaker. Sounds like he hasn't changed much."

"Mom! Please. I don't have time for this. I've got to get in the shower and then go to the airport. Can't we talk about this another time?"

"No. Just what has happened with your contract with Kathleen Armstrong?"

"She had to let me go."

"That's hard to believe."

"It's true."

"And the Richard Lawrence contract?"

"I'm in between jobs and Matt offered me a lot of money to help him out. I couldn't say no." Bridget was talking really fast. He hoped her strategy worked because he felt a sneeze building and didn't know how long he could stifle it.

"Yes, you could. You haven't seen this boy in more than a decade and now every word out of your mouth is Matt this and Matt that. How could you let him interfere with what's important in your life?"

"And what is that?"

"Your modeling career, that's what. It's everything you dreamed about. Everything you worked for. Don't throw it away on a man. I had to give up…"

"Mom, please I've heard the story about how you

got pregnant at sixteen and had to marry Daddy. Then he died and left you alone with a child. Matt's job is only temporary, I promise. The first chance I get I'll go back to modeling. Now, I really have to go. I will call you."

Her mother sniffed and Matt saw her feet turn in the doorway. "I just don't want you to make the same mistakes I did, Bridget."

"Yes, I understand. I'll call you soon."

Mrs. Cole headed for the stairs and he heard their voices get fainter as she walked her mother to the front door.

He wiggled out from under the bed and stood, sneezing and trying to muffle it. Adjusting his disheveled clothes, he intended to join Bridget downstairs. Just as he reached the bottom step, the door swung open and Mrs. Cole entered.

"You! I knew it. I can see where my daughter's head is. I knew you were trouble back then."

"Where's Bridget?"

"Sounds like she's on the phone."

Matt was at a loss as to what to say to Mrs. Cole. Sure he had some choice words for her, but it wasn't the right thing to get between Bridget and her mother.

Mrs. Cole walked up to him and poked him in the chest. "Watch your step, mister. My daughter has plans. So don't think you can mess them up." She gave him one last poke before exiting the house.

Matt rubbed at the spot where she poked. He should heed Mrs. Cole's words. She was right. Bridget wasn't planning to be his CEO forever. It was a temporary situation. But he knew that once she got the business up and running, he could find someone to take over.

Matt swore beneath his breath, regret in his soul. He had been experiencing the best sex of his life and the woman wasn't real. Sure Bridget was flesh and blood, but she would return to her world. The pressure her mother put on Bridget was nothing compared to the enormous pressure Bridget put on herself. And now she was pushing at his carefully controlled life. Getting him mired in a confrontation with her mother, making him lose his focus. He'd gotten into a nice rhythm and letting his passions rule him was not conducive to maintaining and protecting his privacy.

Bridget came back into the room, her hair mussed and her eyes crackling. "I'm so sorry," she said when she saw Matt's face. "What happened?"

"Your mother. Part two."

"Oh God. What did she say?"

"That you had plans and that I couldn't mess them up. So, um, I guess I'll go. Let me know if you need to discuss the business in any way."

Bridget grabbed at his arm and Matt felt the buzz her touch caused all the way down to his groin.

"My mother's a crazy woman, Matt."

"That may be true, but in this respect, I think she's right. Look, we don't need to complicate matters here. You're doing me a favor by building my business. I appreciate that very much."

"What about our friendship? I don't want to lose that again."

"Sure, Bridget. We can be friends, if that's what you want, but I've really got to get back to my research."

She let go of his arm. "I'm sorry, Matt. I know that I came back into your life like a tornado and I really didn't mean to cause you trouble."

Damn, why did the woman have to look so dejected? He just couldn't stand it.

Not thinking of the repercussions, he gathered her against him, holding her tight. "I will always be here for you, Bridget. Who else can you turn to, if you can't turn to your friends?"

"I'm just beginning to realize that, Matt."

She looked up at him and quite literally he was lost in her eyes. It took sheer willpower not to lean down and take that soft, trembling mouth. "You'd better get in the shower if you're going to pick up your consultant. What's that all about, anyway?"

"I needed...help," she said and dropped her eyes as if that was a terribly embarrassing thing to say.

He gently cupped her chin and brought her head back up, thinking how great it was that stoic, image-conscious Bridget was changing right before his eyes. "You seem to think there's something wrong with needing help."

"There is. A person can really only depend on herself. No one makes me. I make myself."

"So what does that mean? That you're not allowed to make mistakes. Dammit, Bridget, your mother's brainwashed you into thinking you have to be perfect all the time. What gives her the right to walk into your aunt's house, come into your room and chastise you about your choices? Don't you give a damn about your privacy? She violates it every time she turns around. It's not right. You should be able to make your own choices without censure."

"I do make my own choices and I resent the fact that you think I don't have any backbone when it comes to my mother. You don't know what I've been through the last twelve years, so don't make judgments you don't understand."

"I understand what's important to you. Making it. That's all there is to you. But do you really know what *it* is? Do you even know what you're pursuing? What you're giving up in the pursuit? When it will be enough?"

She turned her angry face up to his, "I'm going to be late. We'll have to discuss this later." She pulled out of his embrace and headed back upstairs.

Matt stood there for a minute. His anger pulsed through him. Maybe he was beating his head against a brick wall. She couldn't see how her mother's influence was driving her toward something he wasn't sure Bridget knew herself.

It was a losing battle. Keeping his heart distant from Bridget was a fool's errand. He couldn't do it. Lately, she'd never been far from his thoughts. He'd fantasized about every night, too. But the bottom line was that he liked her a whole hell of a lot. Maybe too much. Maybe it bordered on love.

So maybe he couldn't keep his heart distant because she already had it. Bewildered, he turned to go.

Food for thought. He hoped he didn't choke on it.

THE MINUTE BRIDGET saw Naomi emerging from security at Logan, she rushed forward. The fight with Matt fresh in her mind, she needed something else to occupy her thoughts.

She didn't kowtow to her mother's needs and whims. She fulfilled her own desires. Matt didn't know what he was talking about. She cared for him deeply, but it was the same tune he'd played over and over as she was growing up.

Naomi dropped her bag and threw her arms around Bridget.

"It's so good to see you."

"I can't thank you enough...."

"Don't thank me yet. We have work to do."

"Right."

Once in the car, Bridget asked, "How was your flight?"

"Fine. Short."

Bridget stopped at the toll booth and paid.

"Maybe you could explain what kind of hole you've dug for yourself."

"I haven't—"

"Bridget, cut the crap, okay. If we're going to work together, I have to lay some ground rules. First one is no bullshit. You tell me everything. I'm not going to broadcast your personal business to anyone. We're friends, right?"

Naomi's matter-of-fact tone almost made Bridget laugh. "Check. No bullshit." The bright day darkened as they entered the Callahan Tunnel that took them under the Boston Harbor. Bridget didn't like to think how many gallons of water were on top of her as she drove.

"Secondly, I must have a constant supply of caffeine—and no instant. Fresh brewed coffee and keep it flowing."

This time Bridget laughed. "Caffeine, check."

"Hey, coffee is no laughing matter."

"Sure, check, no laughing."

Naomi snorted, losing the cool she was trying to project. "There can be no laughing about coffee. Other forms of mirth are okay."

When they reached the outskirts of Cambridge, Naomi said. "This is the city that is home to Harvard and MIT. It's beautiful."

"I've always loved Cambridge."

Bridget slowed to ease around a MBTA bus dropping off passengers.

She pulled up to her aunt's Victorian and Naomi sighed. "I love the city, but it's so nice to get out once in a while."

"Let's get you settled in the guest room and introduced to my aunt, then there's coffee to brew and work to get done."

"Check," Naomi said and they both laughed.

BRIDGET RUBBED at the back of her neck and glanced at the door as if it were her salvation. She'd been cooped up with Naomi now for one full day. She looked at the clock and it read eleven. They had already incorporated, or more accurately filled out the incorporation paperwork online. Naomi was quite versed on all aspects of incorporation and she had said that Delaware was the perfect state for their new business for many reasons.

They had just finished discussing all the legal ramifications of incorporating, most of which had simply gone over Bridget's head. God, she was tired. She gazed out the window and could see that Matt's light was on in his bedroom. She wondered if he was sleeping or maybe reading. She wondered if he was still mad at her.

"Bridget!"

Bridget turned her attention back to Naomi. "I'm sorry, my mind was wandering."

"I can imagine. But it's time to start on the mission statement."

Bridget groaned.

"I know, this is all cut-and-dried stuff and you've got a creative mind, but it has to be done. Now let's get down to business."

Bridget decided she never wanted to hear those words ever again.

It took them about half an hour to come up with a mission statement. "So the mission of Almost Naked, Inc. is to provide high-quality fabric at a reasonable cost for the manufacturing of high-quality garments offered to consumers. Sounds pretty good," Bridget said.

"Okay, now that we have that, it's time for the business plan."

Bridget bolted for the door and Naomi came after her. "Wait a second. I knew you were going to get squirrelly on me, so I have a proposition for you."

Bridget eyed her with suspicion.

"How about some midnight margaritas and we forget about the business plan until tomorrow?"

Bridget smiled and shoved Naomi. "You are bad. You weren't going to make me do a business plan tonight."

"Nope. That will take us most of the day tomorrow."

"I'm going back to New York and beg every designer there to take me on."

"Come on, Bridget. It won't be that bad."

"Yes it will."

"Think about margaritas for now. Let's go."

They went into her aunt Ida's kitchen and Bridget got out the blender while Naomi pulled the ingredients together.

Naomi said, "When preparing a margarita you only need to know three things: salt/no salt, what style and which alcohol."

"Easy for me. Salt. Frozen. Tequila and triple sec."

"Works for me."

Bridget plugged in the blender and Naomi added the ingredients. Turning it on made a whirring sound, the ice cubes loud in the quiet house.

"I hope this doesn't wake your aunt."

"No, she sleeps like a log."

They poured the drink into glasses and Bridget took her first sip. "Good." She sighed.

Naomi nodded as she swallowed her own drink.

Bridget said, "Hey, let's soak our muscles in the hot tub."

"My bathing suit is upstairs and I don't have the

energy to get it," Naomi said, taking another sip of her drink.

"Who needs a bathing suit," Bridget said with a mischievous grin and proceeded to take off every stitch of clothing.

Naomi went for the kitchen light, giggling like a fool. "What if the neighbors see us?"

"Then we'll turn them on their very proper Bostonian ears, won't we? Come on, Naomi. Live a little."

"Okay." She removed all her clothing and giggled again. "This is crazy."

Bridget went into the laundry room and snagged two fluffy towels from a stack her aunt Ida kept there for use with the hot tub. They went out the back door and it took Bridget a few moments to open the top and turn on the tub.

Bridget and Naomi lowered themselves into the hot water with a sigh. For a few minutes they luxuriated and drank their margaritas.

Finally, Naomi said, "So how's your love life?"

"I hooked up with someone I knew when I was a child. He's sweet. He teaches at MIT."

"Seems like this would be a good town for the brainy types. Lots of black socks, though."

"Is that supposed to make sense to me?"

"I have a new theory about the opposite sex. I like to come up with them every now and again. I feel I need a scorecard to tell if a guy is a winner or a loser. My new theory involves socks."

Bridget had just taken a drink of her margarita.

She sputtered, swallowed some of the concoction and started to cough and laugh at the same time.

"No really," Naomi said as she patted Bridget on the back. "At first, I thought that the way to find out what you wanted to know about a guy was to scrutinize his wardrobe, but sometimes that can be deceptive as anyone could have bought him that stylish jacket. Then I thought his choice in footwear was the key. But this theory is getting harder to prove. It's tough to buy ugly shoes these days, and with the excess of fashionable sneakers everywhere you look, it's pretty hard to figure out what these footwear options may say about their wearer."

"So it's all about socks now?"

"Yes, I think it all comes down to socks."

Bridget laughed. "I see your point. People think that others don't notice their sock choices. Believe me, people, you do have a choice. You really should use your best judgment."

Naomi nodded enthusiastically, grinning like a loon. "Exactly. Take for instance, white socks. They should never be worn with dark pants. They stick out like a neon sign. And, please, athletic socks were not meant to be worn with everything. Doing so shows a lack of style and just plain laziness. Leave them in the gym where they belong."

"My turn," Bridget said, scrunching up her face. "It's anal to match your socks with your dress shoes, and men who match socks with pants show way too much thought about their wardrobe."

Unable to stop laughing, Naomi said, "Tennis socks should only be worn while playing tennis."

Bridget piped in. "And those socks your mother gave you for your birthday with the Garfield print on them should have gone to charity five minutes after you got 'em. Let them go."

Naomi bent over, spasming with laughter. "And, finally, the infamous black socks. I think wearing them shows that the guy is probably very traditional. Unless they are worn with sandals and that's just plain wrong. He probably still lives with his mother."

Between peals of laughter, Bridget said, "I don't know, but have you found the right sock guy?"

"Not quite yet, but I know what I don't like. I guess I'll have to keep searching."

They sat in companionable silence until Naomi polished off her drink. "Look, I'm going to turn in. I'm bushed. I'll come and get you bright and early tomorrow, so don't even try to lock your door."

"Okay."

Naomi grabbed her towel and scooted into the house. Bridget sat in the hot bubbling water letting the kinks bake out of her back and shoulders.

After a few minutes, she heard footsteps and sat upright, reaching for the towel.

"Bridget?" Matt materialized from the darkness and he looked at her naked, glistening body.

She moved to the edge of the tub and looked down, smiling when she saw that Matt didn't wear any socks at all. He was barefoot and sexy.

Softly, Bridget asked, "What are you waiting for?"

7

HE HAD TRIED TO RESIST when he'd seen Bridget's friend head into the house. She hadn't returned and Bridget hadn't gone into the house, either. He looked at his watch and noted it was after midnight, late for a hot tub party.

He chastised himself. Even after their disagreement this morning regarding her mother, he wasn't smart enough to leave her alone and let her get his business off the ground for him.

The more she intruded into his life, the more privacy he lost—but this was Bridget. And the real deal was so much more interesting than the fantasy in his mind.

So now he was standing here while she gazed at him with a soft look on her face and her eyes slightly glazed from fatigue and he would guess alcohol.

What was he waiting for?

Intervention in some form.

"Are you giving me the silent treatment?" She pouted, her generous breasts pressed up against the wooden tub, her blue eyes masked by her thickly lashed lids. "I think you overreacted with my mother."

Matt couldn't answer. The strength of his attraction to Bridget was overpowering.

"Okay, if you're going to stand there and not answer me, could you be a doll and get me another margarita?"

He laughed then and shook his head.

"What is so funny about margaritas, Matt?"

"I'm not laughing at margaritas." He moved forward and took the glass out of her extended hand. "I'm laughing at you."

He heard her huff as he walked away into the house, fighting to get his attraction under control. He picked up the pitcher to see it was empty and proceeded to chuckle some more as he made a fresh batch. Grabbing an extra glass and the blender pitcher, he headed back outside. Just as he got to the door, he stopped and walked back into the laundry room and snagged himself a towel.

He dropped the towel just as he opened the door, and yelped when his head hit the knob as he bent over. Cursing under his breath, he pulled the door shut behind him.

"Serves you right," came her comment from the hot tub.

"Your friend isn't likely to come back out here, is she?"

"No. She went to bed. We spent hours and hours incorporating your business and creating a mission statement."

She glared at him as he poured the margaritas.

That old nursery rhyme came back to him, but he

altered it slightly. Jack went in the house to fetch margaritas. Jack fell down and broke his crown. Much more than that would be broken, if he didn't get his head together.

After the glasses were full, he pulled off his T-shirt and unsnapped and unzipped the same jeans she'd bought him in New York. Truth be told, they were so comfortable, he'd gone out and bought himself two more pairs. When he was naked, he stepped into the tub, the hot water making him sigh as he sat down. Bridget watched him warily. He reached over and grabbed both glasses and handed her one.

"Thanks."

"You're welcome."

"Look, Matt, I'm sorry about what happened this morning with my mother. It must have been embarrassing for you."

She seemed hesitant about getting close to him, and he couldn't stand it. He slipped his arm around her shoulders in a nonchalant way.

"Ever since I came back, I've kicked myself for not staying in touch with you. I felt so detached in New York, like I wasn't substantial, just this hair and smile and…and…body. Full of air, you know, like a balloon."

He pulled her across his lap, unable to help himself. "You feel pretty solid to me."

She closed her eyes and pressed her face into his neck. "That's the nicest thing anyone has ever said to me."

He shook his head and laughed once again. "There you go again."

"What?"

He smiled.

She raised herself up, hanging on to his shoulders. "What is that all about? Are you mocking me now?"

"No, it's just that…you have this way about you that seduces everyone you come into contact with."

Bridget frowned. "Do you think I'm doing it on purpose?"

"No, you would have to be aware of doing…what it is…you do."

"According to you, what I do isn't really my idea. But something that was planted in my mind."

Matt looked down into her stormy blue eyes.

She continued. "I've worked hard to get where I am today. I have a high-powered agent, a New York loft and, mark my words, I will be a supermodel someday."

"Back in New York."

Bridget slid off his lap and moved away. "That's right. I know that you don't think much of the city. You find it noisy and overcrowded. But I see New York as an opportunity and I like the bustle and the craziness of living there."

"You're right. I hate the city and I don't understand why anyone would leave the peace and serenity of Cambridge to go there. But, Bridget, modeling is not everything."

"It is to me. I will get this business off the ground, then I'm going back to New York renewed and refreshed. I'm hoping for a contract from Maggie Winterbourne. I don't intend to come running home with my tail between my legs."

She picked up the margarita glass and drained it. Putting the glass down, she turned to look at him. She licked her lips, leaving them damp and shiny, beckoning for him to nibble and taste.

"Everyone likes a winner, Matt," Bridget said as she moved closer to him. "Admit it. No one likes a loser."

He closed his eyes, trying to maintain his composure. "No. No one likes a loser, but being able to admit that you can't win all the time—that's not the end of the world."

"Shh," she said softly, her thumb stroking over his mouth. "I know what you want, even when you want to deny it."

"What's that?"

"Me, in any position you can get me in."

"I'm not…"

"You're not here to have sex with me, Matt? You don't want it?"

"I'm not immune to you."

"You want it, don't you?"

"Yes."

"See, was that so hard to admit?"

"But it's not…"

"Just sex? Maybe not." The wind picked up, sending a gust of air across her skin. The early June night was warm.

Her nipples automatically puckered and darkened to a deep raspberry hue, and her luminous eyes widened in pleasure.

Her entire body trembled, and her breathing deepened as he stared at her wet skin, fascinated at the way the dewy moisture gathered in places and slowly trickled downward like a soft, misty rain.

God, he'd never seen anything so sexy, so delectably enticing as the mouthwatering feast she presented. Then again she was the first girl he'd ever trusted with his secrets and his heart. And that was both terrifying and a complete turn-on for him. Undoubtedly, Bridget was a pure reckless addiction for his senses, and like a junkie, he intended to get his fill of her.

Aching to caress all that slick glistening flesh, he flattened his palm around the curve of her throat and followed the slick path down to an enticing amount of cleavage. His hands captured her breasts, encircling them with long, possessive fingers and gliding his thumbs across her rigid nipples before he continued on with his lazy journey. Skimming his palms across her quivering belly and down to her smooth sleek thighs, thighs he couldn't wait to feel wrapped tight around his waist.

Bridget moaned, "Matt, please put your mouth on me."

"Where," he rasped out.

"Anywhere," she panted. "Anywhere you want."

He gave in to the need to slide his mouth over her feminine curves, so vibrant and arousing him to the point of dizzying torment. His fingers gradually trailed their way back up her sides, tracing the dip and swell of her hips and waist, stroking the outline of her pale breasts, then finally his hands came to rest on the lip of the tub behind her, surrounding her with the male scent of him, the virile power and heat he emanated, the desire to brand her.

She whimpered at the momentary loss of contact, but he didn't make her suffer long. By slow, agonizing degrees, he closed the scant distance separating their bodies until the hard, masculine contours of his broad chest crushed against her sensitive breasts. Their bare bellies touched, skin searing skin, as he pinned her hips and thighs to the seat of the tub, leaving her no escape.

Their eyes met in the shadowed darkness, and there was no mistaking the hard, solid length of his erection jutting against her mound. He rolled his hips, letting her feel the full effect of that massive ridge, and she reacted with a low, purring sound that sent shivers through him.

"You like that?" he teased.

She widened her legs and arched toward him, silently seeking more. "Oh, yes," she whispered anxiously, and he could see the frustration in her eyes at his slow, mindless seduction.

The dark need inside him was something he always tempered whenever he was with a woman. The deep craving to do things that filled his fantasies, like the thrill of being open and exposed in the night, sent his desire soaring to never before achieved heights. He didn't have to hide with her. As she looked boldly into his eyes, he saw that dark answering hunger in hers. Lowering his head he brushed his mouth across hers. When he slid his tongue against her silky lower lip, she opened her mouth and eagerly let him inside. He deepened the kiss, voracious and hungry, and she answered, sliding her body sensually against his in a rhythm that matched the thrust of his tongue.

One of his hands grasped her gyrating hip while the other slipped over her taut bottom, past her thigh, and he hooked his fingers behind her knee. He lifted her leg up to his waist, wedged his thigh tight between hers, and pressed his groin to her sex, urging her to feel him, all of him.

Every single hard, pulsing inch.

The aching pressure of his cock rubbing against her intimate flesh, along with the friction of the water combined to start her on the exquisite journey to her first climax. He wanted it more than anything. Moving against her caused sensations as exquisite as they were intense, rippling along his cock—undulating waves of passion, beckoning him to push into her as hard as he could. But he refused his body's call, waiting for her. She curled her fingers into his hair as she continued to move sinuously on his muscular thigh until her entire body began to shake. Tearing her mouth from his, she finally took her pleasure with a soft, keening cry of release.

"Yes," he murmured, watching her face, the intense pleasure that he'd given her. "So good."

"I want you inside, Matt, please."

"No, not just yet. Soon."

He slipped his thighs under her, lifting her hips out of the water and setting her on the lip of the tub.

He slid his hands along her sleek thighs and around to her sweet butt. Gently he brought her forward until her legs were wrapped around his chest. Gliding his hands higher, he arched her back, making her groan in anticipation. He pressed his face against the softness of each breast, nuzzling and kissing the plump skin. He dipped his hand into the water and dribbled heated drops onto the tips of her breasts. Bridget writhed against him. Then he grabbed his half-empty margarita glass and poured some of the drink onto those delectable tips. Bridget gasped at the cold alcohol, the nubs tightening into hard knots. He closed his mouth over one tip and sucked the alcohol off. Bridget threw her head back and he moved to the other sweet tip, running his tongue over the taut bead, lapping and swirling until he finally drew that nipple into his mouth and suckled her.

She reached down, taking him into her hand, and her touch charged through his body. Pushing on his chest, she swung him away from her against the lip of the tub until he was sitting fully on the decking surrounding the hot tub. Before he could say a word, she had her hot mouth nipping at his collarbone, trailing down his chest. She found his rigid nipple and bit gently at the sensitive disk, and that stab of erotic sensation spiraled all the way down to his groin.

She kissed her way down his torso to his belly, and kept nibbling her way lower with soft, delicious bites and the scrape of her teeth along his sensitive skin. She took him in her hands, her grasp slick and slippery as she measured the length of his cock in long, heated strokes that had him gritting his teeth in a painful kind of pleasure. Her thumbs grazed the lubricated head of his penis with every pass, drawing a fierce climax closer to the surface.

"Bridget," he said, his voice a deep, husky growl.

She ignored the warning in his tone. She obviously wasn't done tormenting him. Lowering her head, she curled her tongue over the broad head of his sex, then licked and nibbled her way up and down his shaft. Slowly, leisurely, lapped and savored the taste of him with small, appreciative sighs and moans that made him writhe against the tub, just as she had. When he was certain he was on the verge of going insane, she finally parted her lips and enveloped him in the wet heat of her mouth.

His nostrils flared, and lust reared within him as she took him deep, working his thick, solid member with her lips and tongue and the tight fingers wrapped around the base. She brought him to the brink of an orgasm, then eased back to let the wave of sexual tension ebb before starting in on him again.

His entire body shuddered with a fierce, roaring urgency, stunning in its intensity. He couldn't ever remember being the lucky recipient of such intense, all-consuming need. She took her time, delighting in the act and his responsiveness. She skillfully drew out his moment of fulfillment, as if his pleasure was directly linked to her own.

Her tongue swirled one last enthusiastic time, then she sucked, at first gently, then harder, stronger, devouring him all the way to the back of her throat in long, rhythmic strokes of her mouth. He exhaled a hiss of breath, and his arms flexed in an instinctive reaction to reach down and thread his fingers through her hair. When he touched her head, her blond hair was so soft that he groaned.

His stomach muscles clenched and he pressed his hips forward unable to keep the climax at bay. He wasn't going to last much longer. "I'm gonna come, Bridget, if you don't stop."

She didn't stop, and he couldn't. The last thin thread of his control shattered. His hips surged upward as she drew him to completion with her hands and mouth, sending him soaring on the wings of an awesome, shuddering orgasm that left him weak and wasted.

They both sank down into the water, sated and unable to move. After a few moments, Bridget picked up his margarita and downed the rest.

She snuggled up against him.

"You're awesome, Bridget," he whispered, wanting to invite her to his house, drag her down into bed with him and sleep the whole night in each other's arms, but Matt couldn't get the words past his lips. He was too scared to think what that meant. She'd already done so much to shatter any barriers that the thought of having her scent to perfume the air kept his mouth closed.

She didn't protect herself as much as he did. And it still shocked him that her mother had been so intrusive.

But what could he expect? Bridget had been trying to please her mother for a long time and old habits died hard. Even as an adult, she couldn't seem to please herself. Bridget wasn't aware of why she strived so hard to be what her mother wanted her to be. She didn't understand that maybe it wasn't her dream at all.

Everyone made wrong or misguided decisions, along with mistakes they regretted. He had his own burdens to live with, as well—things he wished he could have done differently, like staying in touch with her even though it had been difficult with her mother's intervention.

But he'd learned that he couldn't allow those pitfalls to rule his life, that he had to deal with them and move on. But it appeared that Bridget was still living in the past, for fear of failing the people she cared for the most.

"We should get out of here. You're shivering."

"I don't want to go yet. I want to stay with you."

"You're cold. Come on."

"Party pooper," she groused, but stood up with him when he tugged. He grabbed a towel and draped it around her, tucking it in tightly, securing his own towel around his waist. He walked her to the back door and reached for the handle.

It wouldn't turn.

"What's wrong?" Bridget asked when he tried the knob again.

"It won't open," he replied.

"That can't be," she reached down and tried the knob and realization widened her eyes. She broke into laughter. "You must have accidentally locked it when you hit it with your head."

"This isn't funny, Bridget."

"Yes, it is. Here we are without a stitch of clothing on and my aunt and Naomi are sleeping. What am I going to do?"

She turned to look at him. "I'll have to sleep with you."

"With me?"

"Is that okay?"

"Sure," he said, but inside his mind was churning.

Only a few moments ago he'd been freaked out by the thought of her sleeping in his bed, in his room, but as he looked down into her face with the beaming smile, he knew he'd never deny her anything.

What was happening to him? Deep inside he understood what was happening and he was beginning to realize he was helpless to fight the strong, undeniable feelings she evoked—no matter how much those emotions scared the hell out of him.

"I SEE THAT YOU STILL HAVE your telescope, but you've changed rooms," Bridget said, surveying his space.

"Once my parents left for Arizona, I converted my room into a spare bedroom and moved all my things into the master suite."

"You've renovated in here, too. Didn't your parents have built-in bookshelves?"

"Yeah, they did. I didn't like them. Made this room feel too much like an office. I wanted comfort."

"And privacy. I remember that used to be very important to you."

She walked over to his dresser.

"I need something to wear, Matt."

"Here, let me help you," he offered.

He pulled out a thermal shirt that had shrunk and handed it to her along with the matching pants that now were way too short on him.

"Are you kidding? I don't want to look like I'm wearing hand-me-downs."

"You'll be sleeping."

"Doesn't mean I can't be stylish." She shouldered him out of the way and grabbed a white cotton tank top and a pair of white boxer briefs. She shivered as she dropped the towel, making Matt shift at the sight of her glorious beauty. Even wet and ravished, she looked wonderful.

Bridget pulled the shirt over her head and slipped on the briefs. She looked really good in his clothes, like an expensive ad for men's underwear, making his skin tingle and his mouth water.

She reached up and cupped his face. "Thanks," she said simply. "Do you have a comb I could use?"

"In the bathroom."

She disappeared for a moment and when she emerged the bathroom, every hair was in place, the ends still damp from the hot tub. Walking over to the window, she put her eye to his telescope.

"Wow, look at the stars that are out tonight." He smiled softly, refraining from telling her they were the same stars that were out every night.

"Ooooh, there's the Big Dipper. Looks like it's pouring out dazzling stars."

He stood there and watched her. Unable to help

himself, he reached out and smoothed his hand over her hair. She continued to look at the stars, oblivious to him.

He could remember her standing at his telescope at sixteen, just before her mother limited her trips to her aunt Ida's house. He had wanted so much to kiss her then. Listening to how she was going to be busy for the coming year going to that pageant and this pageant. Matt wished at that moment she hadn't been so blindingly beautiful and he hadn't been so intimidated by her. He would have taken her in his arms and kissed her, told her how he felt about her. But then her mother had called and the moment passed.

Desire began as a slow burn inside him, but not just physical desire. It was the desire to keep this woman in his life because she brightened it like the stars in the heavens. Without her, his world seemed so dark.

She shivered. He stepped behind her and wrapped his arms around her. Leaning back into his warmth, she sighed.

"Point out the constellations to me, Matt."

"There's Ursa Major," he said, obliging her.

"The Great Bear," she said.

"Sagittarius."

"That's easy. The Archer. Where?" she asked.

"Right there," he said, pointing with his arm, tracing the outline of the bow with his pointer finger. "The bow is outlined by three stars—Kaus Borealis forms the northern part of the bow, Kaus Meridionalis forms the middle and Kaus Australis; the southern. The arrow tip is Al Nasl and it forms the point."

"Oh, I see it. This is a much better room to look at the stars, Matt. A better angle. The universe is so vast, it's hard to get your brain around it."

"You're right."

She slipped out of his arms. "You've made this room a wonderful sanctuary. I love the overstuffed chair where you could curl up and think."

She ran her hand over the soft fabric and lifted her head to look at him.

"And this wonderful artwork that you have over the bed. Wow, really erotic."

"The artist is local. Her name is Sheila Bowden and she does nudes using that hazy technique."

"Soft-focus. It's a photographic technique applied to art."

"I like that you can't make out her face."

"You would. You like the fact that she's doing something so bold, yet the fact that her identify remains a mystery is erotic."

He nodded.

"I'm dead on my feet. Would you have a toothbrush I could use?"

Matt froze. It was a simple request, yet seemed so intimate. "Sorry, I only have mine in the bathroom."

"Too bad."

When she closed the bathroom door, Matt walked over to his dresser and pulled out a pair of black boxer briefs and dropped the towel. Slipping on the underwear, he moved over to the bed and pulled the covers down.

He heard the water running in the bathroom and

realized that she was taking a shower. His first thought was to go in there and join her, but it was getting late and he had a full day tomorrow. He sighed and got in under the covers and grabbed his laptop. He did have that paper to finish, one he'd been working on when he'd walked over to the window and saw Bridget running for the hot tub.

He leaned back into the pillows propped against the headboard and focused on the type, just as he heard Bridget singing a song. He couldn't quite make out the words, but her lusty rendition made the corners of his mouth turn up.

The next thing he knew, he'd fallen asleep. Bridget was removing his laptop from his hands and setting it on the bedside table, saving his work, and turning it off.

She pulled the covers over him and walked around to the other side of the bed. When she slipped under the covers, she snuggled up against him, totally invading his personal space like a cat who doesn't know any better. Matt instinctively turned toward her. Gathering her against him, he kissed her sweet mouth.

She deepened the kiss and Matt responded. He was fully aroused in seconds and their joining was fierce and demanding.

8

WITH A SIGH, she opened her eyes and found that she was alone in bed. Disappointed, she rolled to her back and stared up at the ceiling, letting her memory keep her company. At dawn she woke to his mouth on her nipple, as he sucked and swirled his tongue over the sensitive peak. His slow hands on her breasts, his fingers delving to that hot, moist place between her legs drove her crazy with need for him. When his body eased over hers, she enthusiastically widened her legs to accommodate his hips as he sank into her and started to thrust.

This morning's slow and poignant joining was different from last night's quick and fierce mating. Nuzzling her neck, gliding his fingers tenderly through her hair, he'd arched into her so that his cock pressed hard and perfectly against her erogenous zone. He'd captured her gaze, locking his eyes on her as he absorbed every pleasurable nuance that flitted across her face. He'd orchestrated her orgasm, building it slowly, intensifying it into a tingling, magnificent sensation that crested through her in surging waves of ecstasy. He came with her on a long, low groan that vibrated his chest against hers.

What a glorious way to greet the day.

She massaged her way down each hard muscle of his back, sliding over the taut slope of his ass and said softly in his ear, "I should go."

"It's only five and you're still locked out. Get some more shut-eye." His lips brushed against her mouth and when she opened for his deep kiss, he moaned softly. He withdrew from her soft, satiated body. "I'll walk you back later."

She'd been unable to resist his sweet, caring suggestion to rest a bit longer, and burrowed beneath the warm blanket and comforter. She heard him get up and take a shower, but she was too tired and satiated to start the day just yet. She'd drifted back into a deep, dreamless sleep. And now, as she glanced at the digital clock on the nightstand, she realized it was a quarter past eight, when she was normally up by six a.m. to start her day.

She wasn't worried about her aunt, since she would have already gone to work, but Naomi would be looking for her just as she promised.

Throwing back the covers, she sat up and stretched, shivering as the cool morning air hit her bare skin. To her surprise, she found a pair of her own jeans, a long-sleeved deep amethyst silk blouse and a short denim jacket along with a bra and panties to match the deep purple of the blouse. He'd also included a pair of her delectable Jimmy Choo sandals. How much more could she stand? He was too thoughtful, a trait clearly lacking in any of her boy-friends. Making her way to the bathroom, she took care of business. Catching a glimpse of herself in the mirror, she cringed. She looked like the Wicked Witch of the East's ugly sister. Picking up Matt's comb she worked on getting her hair back into its sleek style, and then scrubbed her face and body clean. Back in the bedroom, she slipped into the soft cotton bra and thong, pulled on the jeans and but-toned up her shirt.

A tightness closed her throat and started a deep ache in her heart. The affection and hunger only in-tensified with each encounter with Matt. It was as if she gave a little part of herself to him each time they were together, each time they had sex.

Last night had been a hot, uninhibited display of out-of-control sex. But the mood this morning had been one of tenderness and warmth—making love in the deepest, most profound way. Staggered and stunned by the insight, and feeling devastatingly vul-nerable, she pressed a hand over her swiftly beating heart, working hard to curb the emotions causing an uproar within her. Emotions she was helpless to deny.

But how she felt about Matt didn't change any-thing—not their business deal or their temporary relationship.

Feelings were like speed bumps—they just slowed her down.

With the reminder fresh in her mind, she gathered her composure and headed downstairs.

When she reached the living room and made her

way to the kitchen, Matt was nowhere to be found. She heard a noise downstairs and saw an open door. Perhaps he was in his basement.

She started down the stairs, and then paused when she heard his voice. "Bridget?"

"No, it is I, master, Igor."

He chuckled and said, "Stay there. I'll be right up."

She turned around, heeding the warning in his voice that she was way too close to his innermost sanctum. Matt was a stickler for privacy and it was a somewhat irksome trait. What could she possibly disturb down there?

He came up the stairs and Bridget peeked around his shoulder. "Afraid I'll touch something?"

"What?"

"You don't want me downstairs, right?"

"It's just my office. I'm sure you really wouldn't be that interested."

"I'm interested in anything you do, Matt. I don't get this prickly thing."

He stiffened and moved past her on the stairs. "It's just an office. I'm not making Frankenstein's monster down there."

"Now, that would be interesting, indeed."

He stood at the entrance into the kitchen. "Are you coming, Igor?"

"No. I'd better go. Naomi will be looking for me with the ropes and chains."

"Okay. I'll walk you over."

"Thanks. How did you manage to get my clothing?"

"I knocked on your door. Your aunt didn't blink

an eye. I went up to your room and got the things for you. Luckily your friend was still asleep."

When Bridget got to her aunt's door, Naomi threw it open and said firmly, "If you think you're going to get out of…oh, sorry." She paused when she saw Matt. Reaching out her hand, she said, "Hi, I'm Naomi Carlyle."

"Matt Fox," Matt responded and clasped her hand.

"You sure are."

"Naomi, he's paying your fee."

"Oops. Not the best way to make a good first impression."

Matt smiled easily. "Don't worry about it. Thanks for the compliment." Matt turned toward her and his eyes were earnest. "I've got to get back to work. And no more margaritas."

Bridget rubbed at her temples. "Yes, boss."

"What a hunk and he's an MIT professor, too? Brains and brawn." Naomi sighed as they watched him walk to his front door. "Whew, those are some nice credentials," she said, eyeing Matt's butt. "I suppose you've got him tagged?"

"Tagged and bagged."

"Figures," Naomi said with a pout. She gave Bridget a sideways look, a mischievous twinkle in her eyes. "So what kind of socks does he wear?"

Bridget sighed. "Who cares."

BRIDGET AND NAOMI had been working for three hours before Bridget called a stop. The business plan was much more involved than the mission statement.

"I can't take one more goal nor do one more chart until I get a break," Bridget said, easing toward the door.

"Let's go out to lunch and do some shopping. You can show me around Cambridge," Naomi said with a grin. "I've been here two days and all I've seen is my nice accommodations."

Bridget stopped and eyed her friend. "Really? You're not going to slave drive me into finishing this plan?"

"It can wait. I'd love to see the city and I've never been to Boston before. All that time in New York, you'd think I could get up here for one weekend."

Bridget led the way out of the office. "I never did ask where you were from originally."

Bridget grabbed her stylish cropped black quilted jacket, handing Naomi her denim jacket. "Wisconsin. Always dreamed of living in the big city as some buttoned-up stockbroker, but then I got my degree and I just couldn't seem to get interested in working for Wall Street. Went into business for myself and I love it. Although, what you're doing here is something exciting. Something I would leave my practice for."

"Nobody said you couldn't stay and help me."

"Ha."

Bridget opened the door of her aunt's sporty BMW and slid into the driver's seat. She headed toward downtown and her favorite seafood restaurant, The Lobster Claw.

"Your aunt is as great as you said she was."

"I feel so guilty. I've been here going on three weeks and we haven't even talked that much."

They ordered lunch at the casual seafood restaurant overlooking the Charles River and shared a platter of clams, sautéed shrimp, steamed mussels and crab legs.

Bridget took a drink of the iced tea she'd ordered, and glanced at Naomi. "So, Wisconsin is famous for cheese, right?"

"I'm from a town called Two Rivers. It's on the eastern side of the state bordering on Lake Michigan. Ferries dock there and it takes about nine hours to cross the lake to Illinois."

"I am so clueless about the Midwest."

Naomi said, "So you grew up here. What was that like?"

"It's a quaint little town and very scholarly. My stepfather teaches at Harvard. How about your father?"

A muscle flexed in Naomi's jaw and her expression turned speculative. "My dad owns a cheese factory and produces a lot of cheese. You can't imagine how good it tastes just after it's been cured." She dipped a clam in cocktail sauce and brought it up to her mouth to eat, then licked the excess condiment from her fingers. "If we were in Wisconsin right now, we'd be eating fried cheese curds in a great restaurant called Friar Tuck."

"Those are good, huh?"

"Delicious."

Bridget swirled the last shrimp in garlic-butter sauce and lifted it to her lips.

Wiping her mouth on a napkin, she motioned their waitress back to the table, since they'd pretty much cleared their platter. She waited while the young woman removed their dishes. Naomi ordered two pieces of decadent strawberry-covered cheesecake.

Once the waitress had moved on to fill their dessert order, Naomi said, "What does your father teach at Harvard?"

"English literature. What does it take to cure cheese, anyway?"

"Bridget, would you rather we had more of a business relationship?"

Bridget looked at Naomi and then looked down. "No, why do you say that?"

"I've noticed that you don't really want to talk about yourself."

"You have to let me get used to this friendship thing. I travel and work so much, I'm not used to it. Most of the people I meet aren't really interested in much except how I look. But I really do want to change that." The truth of the matter was it was still difficult to let herself go, even realizing that she wanted to be friends with Naomi. Bridget wiggled her shoulders to loosen them up.

"I think I can handle that. I haven't met many people in New York that I'd want to hang out with on a regular basis."

Naomi waited until the waitress served their dessert before she continued. "I have other models as clients. Do you think I want to be friends with any of them?"

Bridget picked up her fork and dug into the cheesecake. "Why wouldn't you?"

"They don't seem to bother with niceties. You know how it is when you're running from job to job.

I think it's a defense mechanism to keep from making friends you can't share time with."

"I have somewhat of the same problem."

"But you're different, Bridget. You don't dispense with the niceties. I bet you would have won Miss Congeniality if you hadn't been crowned Miss National."

"How did you know about that?"

"Saw *On* magazine on the plane. How was it to be the most beautiful and poised woman in the nation?"

"Scary and exhilarating. The travel was wonderful, but I was glad to settle down in one place after that whirlwind year. I so enjoyed all the people I met and all the charities I was able to help. After my year was up, I had the modeling contract to fall back on and I even got a screen test for a Hollywood movie. Didn't pan out."

"Have you given up on modeling?"

"No. The job with Matt is temporary."

"So what's the dish about our dishy boss?"

"We're doing business together."

"Your business with him happens to include early-morning walks?"

"Not exactly." Walking really had nothing to do with it. Bridget couldn't get the euphoric feeling of that early-morning sex to dissipate.

Naomi must have caught the dazed look on her face, because she leaped on it with interest. "It appears that you two have more than business going on." She tilted her head and perused Bridget speculatively, then grinned. "You slept with him last night, didn't you?"

She trusted Naomi now, unconditionally, in fact.

"Yeah, I did. He accidentally locked me out and I had to sleep over at his house."

"Way to go." Naomi stared at her with visible glee.

Bridget shrugged, playing it down. "I'll be going back to New York when his business gets established. I intend to get myself another lucrative contract. So, it's nothing serious." As long as she kept those pesky emotions from getting to her.

"Nobody said it had to be," Naomi said pragmatically but with genuine caring. "Just enjoy yourself, and Dr. Fox, for as long as it lasts."

Now that was something she could easily agree with. "I intend to."

"But you have to answer one question for me." Naomi leaned toward her and lowered her voice secretively, obviously trying to keep her question just between them and out of earshot of any customers. "How was he in bed?"

Memories of just how good he was filtered through Bridget's mind and her heart picked up its beat, making her feel like a teenager with a crush. "He was…unbelievable." It was the only word she could think of to describe Matt Fox and do him justice. "He is the best lover I've ever had." And he had the wonderful ability to let himself go when he was with her, an uninhibited male in the sack, full of passion and fun.

Naomi really didn't have to know all the details, just as Matt didn't have to know everything there was to know. She had to keep her wits about her and not lose herself in the heat of him.

"So, what's the next plan of action?" Naomi said, snagging the check before Bridget could and smiling.

"I've been thinking about that and I have an idea, but now it's time to shop. I saw a pair of Maggie Winterbourne heels that have my name on them."

"You can take the girl out of New York, but thank God you can't take New York out of the girl. Lead the way."

BRIDGET TRIED ON the wonderful black suede cage-style straps with the four-inch heels.

"Those shoes are beautiful on your feet," Naomi said.

"Well, what do we have here?" a tall brunette drawled with interest and a flash of humor. "I didn't know they allowed riffraff in this classy place."

Bridget met the clear aquamarine of the woman's eyes, a smile turning up the corners of her mouth. She was with a stunning redhead who smiled at Bridget. Memories flooded back of the hectic pace of beauty pageants, the anything-for-the-crown mentality and the friends she'd made. Softly she said, "Well, if it isn't the original Steel Magnolia, Betty Sue Dawkins."

"Fancy meeting you here. Looks like the highfalutin Bridget Cole has come home to roost. Come here, gal. I haven't seen you in a month of Sundays."

Bridget hugged Betty Sue and then turned to Naomi. "Betty Sue, this is Naomi Carlyle, a friend from New York. Betty Sue and I were contestants in the Miss National pageant. She was first runner-up."

Betty Sue nodded, adjusting the thin strap of her designer purse over her shoulder.

"What are you doing in Cambridge?" Bridget asked.

"My husband, Harley, he teaches at Harvard. He's older than dirt, but I love him," she drawled, her eyes sparkling with humor. "Hey, if you have the time, sugah, why don't you come on over to one of our BQU meetings?"

"BQU?"

"Beauty Queens Unite."

"What is your mission statement?" Bridget asked, giving Naomi a sidelong glance and a grin.

"We solemnly swear to bitch and moan as long as possible on one subject for each meeting. One of our most likely subjects is men. In fact, Daphne here, she's a former cheerleader or as we like to call her an Athletic Beauty Queen. Same diff. Anyhoo, the first time she comes to a meeting, I say, 'Find you another one.' Daphne says, 'Excuse me?' and I say, 'I can see that you're pining over a man. Not worth it. As my daddy always says, they're a dime a dozen. Find you another one.'"

All four women laughed and Bridget said, "Sounds like a great topic. Where do you meet?"

"At my house. Right now we have about six Queens. There's two actual Pageant Queens, me and a sweet little thang who got cut from the Miss National pageant. Never made it on TV, poor thang. Then there's Daphne, of course. She's our only Athletic Queen. Then we have a Mall Queen and, believe me, you will shop till you drop, or she'll know the reason why. We have our own African Queen and she's teaching all us tight asses how to walk with attitude. Last but not least a Drag Queen and he's got great fashion and makeup tips. Makes for interesting meetings."

"I'd love to come. I'm sure it'll be fun."

"Bring your friend along, she looks like she's got a little Queen in her."

9

"HEY, WHAT IS ALL THIS?" Naomi asked as she walked into the living room still dressed in her pj's.

"This is my brainstorm. We're going to send out swatches to all the designers and the fabric buyers." Bridget had been up since five, so excited about her plan of action she couldn't sleep. She'd also felt completely guilty about the fact that Naomi had finished up the business plan alone yesterday. After shopping and her reunion with Betty Sue, she hadn't been able to get her mind back to the boring details.

Instead, she'd thought about how optimistic she'd been when she'd been crowned Miss National, all the attention she'd received and all the good she'd done while wearing the crown. Oh, the plans she'd had and she'd followed through on most of them. She had become a successful model.

Now she wished she had paid more attention to saving for a rainy day instead of living the lavish New York lifestyle. If she had, she would have had something to fall back on when she'd lost her contract with Kathleen. That pesky hindsight.

"That's a great idea, but you should have asked me for help," Naomi said.

"You finished up the business plan because I was a whiner. I let you sleep in, but if you want to help, dig in."

"Let me go shower and change and I'll be right down."

Bridget gave Naomi a thumbs-up sign. Naomi was a gem and Bridget was thankful that she had her. But as she looked around at all the work she'd accomplished that morning, she realized that she had invested herself in Matt's business. It was now a matter of pride that she do the best job possible. Sure, she hadn't been sure when she'd agreed to start up the business for him how much work would be involved. But now it was important for her to make this business a success. Not because it would make her look good, but because she cared so much about Matt.

There was a knock on the front door and Bridget went to open it. Matt was standing on the threshold.

"Hi, come in."

"Thanks," he said. "I was wondering if you'd be interested in going to a gallery showing tonight of Sheila Bowden's work. Maybe we could catch a bite to eat."

Bridget felt the warmth seep into her. "Are you asking me on a date, Dr. Fox?"

He looked down and shuffled his feet. "I guess so. I really think you'd like the gallery."

She moved closer to him and he smiled, looking around. "Is your aunt gone?"

"She's at work, but Naomi's upstairs," Bridget said, unable to resist running her hands through his cute, spiky hair. The texture against her hand warmed her with anticipation and a fluttery desire. When her palm slid against the hot skin of his neck, he gasped and she lifted up slightly to reach his warm, sweet mouth.

Unable to help herself, she deepened the kiss, her mouth insistent. He leaned into her just as helpless as she, meeting the press of her mouth. Matt abruptly pulled back when the water went off upstairs. "Too bad you're not alone, but we'll make up for that later."

At that husky promise in his voice, the tingly, fluttery warmth turned hard and taut, making her breath catch. "Come on, I've got something to show you."

She took his hand and drew him into the living room.

"Damn." He reached down and picked up one of Bridget's white cards with samples of his fabric stapled to the front. The card had the content, fiber, care, cost per yard, item number and colors on it.

"You're really moving forward with this idea."

"You'll get a good return on your investment, Matt. I promise."

"You're really going back to New York."

The harsh sound of his voice spoke more than the simple words. He waited, oddly tense, for her answer.

"Yes," she said, stapling on three swatches of cloth to another piece of white index stock paper.

"What if you can't find a job?"

When she saw the intensity in his eyes, her heart skipped a beat. She picked up the labels she'd printed out on her aunt's computer and peeled one off. Setting it firmly below the swatches, she looked up at him, her chest tight. "I will. It's just a matter of time."

"Have you thought about doing something else?"

"Why do you keep pushing that, Matt? Modeling is what I do. Do you think it's beneath me?"

"It isn't beneath you. I didn't mean it that way." He squatted down so that he was at her eye level. "I think that you should weigh all your options. What do *you* really want to do?"

Denial burst inside her. She would go back to modeling. She would not fail. Oh damn, she couldn't fail. If she did, she'd have to admit that all she had strived for all of her life had been for nothing. Meant nothing. She had nothing to show for all her years of hard work. "I'm not ready to accept defeat, Matt."

"I knew he was trying to talk you out of what is best for you."

Bridget and Matt turned toward the door. Bridget's mother was standing there.

"This is a private conversation," Matt said coldly, rising from his crouched position.

"What involves my daughter, involves me," her mother said, eyeing Matt as if he was a dangerous enemy and Bridget supposed that, in her mother's eyes, he was.

Matt was not at all intimidated and Bridget remembered how he had stood up to bullies without fear when he'd been a child. His protective behavior touched something deep inside her and settled there, making her more than a little panicked. The dislike in her mother's eyes was tangible, but Matt never even flinched. As they squared off, Bridget's panic was replaced by a tangle of other emotions.

He crossed his arms over his chest. "In case you haven't noticed, Bridget's a grown woman and can make her own choices."

Bridget sighed. He couldn't have said anything truer. She needed to exert that control right now before they started a feud in earnest. She touched Matt's arm to get his attention and to ease some of the tautness of his muscles. "That's right, Matt," she said pointedly, and he was smart enough to look sheepish. "I can make my own choices." She turned to her mother. "Mom, to what do we owe the pleasure of your visit?"

"I wanted to invite you to my Ladies Social Club gathering—a garden party." She looked at Matt. "You can bring him if you want to, although I doubt he'll enjoy it."

"I'm not sure that he'll…"

"I'll go," Matt said, the line of his jaw tense.

"But, Matt…"

"I said I'll go. Just let me know when and where. I'll talk to you later, Bridget. I should get to school. I meet with my lab staff on Friday."

Bridget rubbed the back of her neck. "I'll call you to get the particulars for tonight. We're still on, right?"

He smiled and nodded. "Have a nice day, Mrs. Cole."

· She harrumphed as he passed, but Matt didn't rise to the bait.

"What do you see in that man? I'll never understand it. He thinks he's so high and mighty because he has a college degree and a doctorate and you don't."

"He does not, Mother."

"I think he looks down his academic nose at you, Bridget. You should really think about what would happen if he talks you into staying here and quitting modeling."

"What do you have against Matt, Mom?"

"He's just like your stepfather."

"Matt's nothing like him."

"He isn't? Has he invited you to any faculty functions or invited you to campus?"

"No, but that doesn't mean anything."

"Doesn't it? I've lived with the disapproval of a man who thinks what I do is frivolous. I don't want you to make the same mistake. Matt's in academia. He doesn't understand the world you live in."

"I know that we come from different worlds, but you're wrong about Matt."

"I hope you don't have to test that theory, Bridget."

"Don't worry, Mom. I'll make sure that your sacrifice means something." The words were out of her mouth before Bridget could stifle them, a bitterness rising in her.

Her mother's face pinched into a disapproving frown. "Go ahead and mock me, but Cambridge is a dead end. New York is where you belong. I'll see you at the garden party a week from Saturday at twelve-thirty sharp."

Her mother's words stung and tears welled in Bridget's eyes. She hadn't realized that those words were in her. Had she been trying to live a life her mother wanted instead of her own life? Her breath caught as she groped for the chair and lowered herself into it. Her heart pounded in her chest, part of the adrenaline rush she got at the thought that maybe this wouldn't have been the life she would have chosen for herself. Maybe she had been pushed and prodded and ordered into pageants and modeling had seemed like the most logical next step, but was it what she wanted?

Bridget suddenly realized that she didn't really know what it was she wanted. A dark void opened up inside her making her heart beat just that much faster. It was too scary to look into that void and try to create something to fill it. Of course she was on the right path. She'd been doing this since she was six for crying out loud. It had to be the right choice. If she quit now, she failed. She owed it to herself to make a second chance and go out a success. Maybe then she could think about what else might work for her.

She squeezed her eyes shut, willing away the tears and the hard lump of emotion filling her throat.

She took a deep breath, calming her nerves. Turning to look, Bridget knew she couldn't get all this work done in one day, even with Naomi's help. She walked into the hall and picked up her purse, digging inside for Betty Sue's number.

She had a fleeting thought that, in the past, she would never have reached out for help, but her friendship with Naomi had taught her that asking for help wasn't the same as failing. Friendships were rich and powerful, full of sharing and kindness, and care. She decided that it was something she could very easily get accustomed to.

She smiled as she dialed. The BQU would come to her rescue.

And they came en masse, all six—five women and one very beautiful man. They pitched in while Naomi made coffee and supervised.

The man, a drag queen named Danny, did three shows on Saturday in a club in Boston. He entertained them with imitations of Barbara Streisand and Liza Minnelli. Bridget had to clutch her stomach and try to breathe through the laughter.

After about an hour of working, Danny said, "Bridget, honey. Where did you get that blouse? It's just simply divine." All the other BQU members nodded and exclaimed that they had to know where they could buy one.

Bridget, stunned, replied, "You can't buy it in a store. I made it out of the fabric you're stapling to those cards."

"So what pattern did you use then? I'm a whiz at sewing," Danny said.

Feeling heat suffuse her face, Bridget, said, "I didn't use a pattern. I designed it myself."

"Well, honey, you're in the wrong business," Danny said. "You shouldn't be wearing the clothes. You should be designing them."

Bridget shook her head and laughed. "No. Not me. It's just something I tried. It's not that big a deal."

"Oh, honey. I'm here to tell you that you'd rake in the cash if you made more of those. In fact, could you make me one?"

"I could make you one if you really like it. It's the least I can do for all your help today. The fabric is so comfortable."

"That would be peachy, honey. Thanks."

MATT COULDN'T TAKE his gaze off the gorgeous, breathtaking woman walking down the stairs.

She quite literally took his breath away.

He'd expected her to look good. Bridget always looked good, but the shimmering, tight black dress she wore was stunning, combined with the artfully applied makeup that enhanced her blue eyes yet didn't overwhelm her beautiful features. Her blond tresses were swept up into a soft, sensual style that showed off her neck, the line of her jaw and gave him access to plenty of bare flesh—from her shoulders all the way down to the base of her spine. Then there were those sexy black strappy heels she wore that made her stocking-clad legs look impossibly long and slender.

But, as centerfold-seductive as she looked, it was the sweet, wholesome, down-to-earth woman beneath all the outer trappings who drew him the most, and always would. And as her gaze met his in the dimly lit interior of the hall, he felt his heart go into a free fall.

He picked up her hand, those red polished nails of hers turning him on. "You are breathtaking."

Her beautiful mouth, tinted in a delicious glossy shade of honey, curved. "Thank you...for the compliment and the invitation. I've forgotten how much fun it is to play dress up."

Grinning, he stroked his thumb along the pulse in her wrist. "You're welcome, for the compliment and the invitation."

Matt offered his arm and she giggled and took it. "Such a gentleman."

Her aunt poked her head out of the kitchen and said, "Have a good time, dear."

"Thanks," Bridget replied as Naomi materialized beside her eating an apple. "Wow. You look fab. Those sandals are great with that dress."

"What are you going to do tonight? No work, I hope," Bridget said.

"Nope. I'm going to beat your aunt at gin. Isn't that right, Ida?"

"That's Aunt Ida to you, upstart, and we'll just see about that." Her aunt winked at Bridget and Matt steered her out the door.

Bridget stopped at the curb and smiled. "You drove the coupe. There is a wild man in there somewhere. Admit it."

"I admit that the car drives like a dream and is addicting. Money is good for something."

"Nice to know that you're affected by material things in life, Matt. Makes you more..."

"Human."

"No, like the rest of us. Shallow."

"You're not shallow, Bridget."

She gave him a sidelong glance as he opened the car door for her. "I was kidding."

"Oh."

After settling her in, he walked around the car and lowered himself into the driver's seat. The thrill of the powerful engine under his control never ceased to excite him. "How did the swatch project go today?"

"I got it done with help."

He turned his head briefly and noticed that one of the black straps of her dress had slid down her creamy shoulder. He braked at a light. Reaching over, he grasped the silky material and slid the strap ever so slowly back up.

"Thank you." Her sultry voice was laced with the same desire shining in her eyes.

He let his fingers linger, tracing a path to the sensitive nape of her neck. He stroked his fingers along her throat and watched with pleasure as her breasts quivered and her nipples peaked against the fabric. Unable to help himself, he brushed his palm over one taut bud and Bridget gasped in the dim interior of the car.

A horn beeped and Matt reluctantly broke eye contact and started to move forward to appease the driver behind him.

He parked in the gallery lot, and they walked hand in hand through the front doors of Studio 10. The building housed nine other studios, starting with the number one and ending with the upscale gallery taking up all of the ground floor.

Inside there was a soft glow of light, along with a number of people mingling in a cocktail-party-type atmosphere. Many were holding champagne and wineglasses as they walked among the paintings, sculpture and art objects that were displayed on pedestals on the floor and hanging on the walls.

Bridget snagged two glasses of champagne from the waiter passing by and handed one to him. He was sucked into a contemplative discussion with a rotund man Matt didn't know about a large ball of marble and what the artist's vision could have been. Bridget sauntered off. He surreptitiously watched her, noting how she was in her element, working the room like a pro. He watched people laugh and so easily fall under her enchanting spell. Matt was content to stay in one place and take in the people, the art and the atmosphere, while Bridget wanted to involve herself in the mix. After a conversation with a tall brunette dressed in a stunning blue gown, they moved over to the Sheila Bowden collection hanging on a far wall.

Bridget got into an earnest conversation with the woman and soon she was searching the room for him. Wondering what she was cooking up in that blond head of hers, he met her gaze. Excitement crackled in the blue depths of her eyes as she motioned him over. When he reached her, Bridget turned to the tall woman and introduced him. "Matt, this is Sheila Bowden. Matt's a great fan of your work. He has one of your nudes over his bed."

"Does he? A fine connoisseur of artwork, then," she said in a soft British accent.

"I like your work very much."

"Matt, Sheila has invited us up to look at her studio. She has number seven."

"This isn't an imposition, Ms. Bowden?"

"Of course not, ducks, and please call me Sheila. Let's go."

Walking to a side door in the large expanse of the gallery, Sheila produced a key and unlocked the door. It led to a staircase and to her studio.

She opened that door, too, and flipped on the light, standing aside to let them in. It was a large room with numerous canvases standing against one wall. The thick smell of paint permeated the air along with the lingering aroma of strong coffee.

The walls were painted in a soft blue hue, the ceiling open beams and the floor hardwood. A chaise in a bright Mediterranean blue was situated near the back wall, a cozy nook for relaxing.

Sheila walked over to a long table where her art supplies were stored and picked up a pad and a charcoal pencil. Bridget walked over to the chaise.

"Bridget, would you mind taking off your dress and posing for me now?"

Before Matt could blink, she slipped the straps of the black dress off her shoulders, over her generous bare breasts until the soft material lay in a silky pool around her feet. Bending down, she retrieved the dress, smoothed out the material and laid the garment over the chaise. She bent over to remove the sandals, but Sheila said, "No, leave them and the thigh highs, too. For now, anyway."

Matt shifted, backing up until he hit the wall. He looked over at Sheila, who was studying Bridget's form with the eye of an artist. "I can see why you were a model, Bridget. You have the most perfectly proportioned body," Sheila said as she grabbed the stool and dragged it closer to the chaise.

Bridget looked over at Matt. "Isn't this exciting? She said she wanted to draw me."

Exciting wasn't the word that first came to mind. It was awkward to be present in the room, but as time passed and Sheila positioned Bridget into a profile pose, Matt couldn't stop his eyes from roaming over her, his embarrassment replaced by a slow burn inside him.

He envied her natural abandon as Sheila touched her arm and turned Bridget's shoulder, as Bridget nodded at Sheila's instructions. Matt's eyes roved over Bridget, her high, pert breasts thrust out, the nipples a raspberry hue under the soft lights. Her slender rib cage flowed to her small waist and slim flaring hips, tapering down to exquisitely long legs, taut thighs and muscular calves. His eyes caressed her fine ass, firm twin globes.

Matt's breath caught as a sudden realization came to him. This was her—all wild abandon and bold display, so very different from him. He knew in that sudden moment that he loved her, desperately. She would go back to New York to pursue her dream and how could he stop her? He was a small blip on her radar, a fun time in Cambridge while she gathered her defenses and prepared for another assault on the fashion industry.

He closed his eyes as sudden pain rushed into his hard-beating heart. He'd *always* been in love with her and he was smart enough not to try to deny it. He loved her from afar as a teenager and now that he'd had the pleasure of loving her close up as a man, he felt bereft that she would walk away.

He didn't know how to hold her, fit her into his life or how he could ever fit into hers. He knew he would lose her, had to trap this desperate love inside and keep it hidden. It was the only way he knew how to function. She could never know, never pity him.

Bridget looked at him then and smiled. In his state of mind, he wasn't prepared for the well of emotion that spiked in him. It overwhelmed him. She reached out her hand and said, "Matt, come over here. Sheila wants us to pose for her."

Together.

No. He wasn't prepared for this. She didn't even ask his permission. He didn't put himself out there on a whim.

He had to think.

He needed air, felt as if he was suffocating on the intense feelings he had for Bridget. He stopped sideways, the small of his back hitting the doorknob with a stab of pain. He reached blindly back and opened it, sliding out into the hall where he took a deep, gasping breath.

She just didn't understand his need for privacy. He

should have realized that his desire for Bridget would mislead him and make him lose his control.

She was the only woman who could do that, make him forget about everything. He retreated down the stairs, back through the gallery and into the street. The summer air refreshed him.

He'd wait for her here, his thoughts in turmoil.

He didn't think his intellect was going to get him out of this one. Even now he wanted to be immersed in her and in the next minute he wanted to run like hell.

But he couldn't run. It was too late.

10

WHEN HE OPENED THE DOOR to the studio, Bridget had wrapped herself in a white sheet. She was looking at the sketch Sheila Bowden had in her hands. Their heads turned as he came back into the room.

"There you are," Sheila said. "I have to go back downstairs to attend to my guests. You can stay here as long as you need, Bridget," she said, giving Matt a telling look.

Matt didn't even notice when she left and the door closed behind her.

"I did something wrong," she said.

"I can't do what you do. Taking off my clothes without any preparation is just beyond me."

"Oh. I'm sorry," she said in a cool little voice he'd never heard her use before. Not with him, not with anybody.

His mouth tightened. His heart hurt.

Resignation, when he'd grown accustomed to sass.

Oh, he didn't like this voice. It broke his heart.

Wearing nothing but the flimsy sheet and the skin he couldn't get enough of stroking, she just stared at him, not moving, waiting for him.

"I know you are," he whispered. "Our lives have changed so much since we were sixteen. I wonder what would have happened if your mother hadn't interfered."

"We'll never know, Matt. We have to deal with now. With these feelings we have for each other and reality. I wish things were different, but we want different things and I'm not sure that can be worked out."

"Maybe. Maybe not. All I know is that you are an amazing woman. You make me want to be a different man, one who puts himself on the line for what he believes in, regardless of the consequences. I don't know if I have that in me."

"Not everyone can change, some people just don't want to. They like where they are. I would never force you to change who you are, Matt."

He nodded. He should tell her right now that he loved her, but was afraid of what that meant. Afraid to move forward because of the unknown. Matt always protected what he held dear. He cherished his quiet and his solitude. Bridget was the only person to ever make him want to break out of those safe old habits. Fear welled in him. He liked having his safety net and this relationship with Bridget didn't have one. He was too afraid of taking that first step. He was happy in his research, his well-known routines that grounded him. If he spoke his feelings out loud, it would lead to change. And change had consequences.

"What we have is so very special to me. The connection we had as kids has grown to something richer and more beautiful. I will always cherish this time we've had together," she said.

"So will I."

Cupping the back of her head, he gathered her up in a tight embrace, his hand tangled in her hair. Shifting so she was flat against him, he shut his eyes, the rush of sensation so intense that he had to grit his teeth against it. He tightened his hold on her, his heart hammering, his breathing constricted. She moved, sending a shock wave of heat through him, the feel of her almost too much to handle in the aftermath of his discovery that he'd loved her for so long.

His fingers snagging in her hair, he tucked his head against hers, forcing himself to remain immobile. Every muscle in his body demanded that he move, and his nerve endings felt as if they were stripped raw, but he tried to ignore the feelings pounding through him. She had no idea what she was doing to him, but he was all too aware of what was happening.

It took him a while, but he finally got himself under control, and he could finally breathe without it nearly killing him. Releasing a shaky sigh, he adjusted his hold on her, drawing her deeper into his embrace, his lungs constricting. The thought that he hurt her made his heart clench hard in his chest.

He tightened his arms around her and simply held her, the fullness in his chest expanding. She was so damned beautiful to him. And vulnerable. She had needed him desperately when she'd showed up in Cambridge and once again, he'd been there for her.

It gave him a jolt to realize that he'd been so glad it had been him.

Unable to control the urge, he widened his stance a little, pressing her against his hard ridge of flesh beneath the fly of his dress pants, turning his face against her neck and clenching his teeth.

She went still in his arms; then she made a low, desperate sound and twisted her head, her mouth suddenly hot and urgent against his. The bolt of pure raw sensation knocked the wind right out of him. Matt shuddered, and he widened his mouth against hers, feeding on the desperation that poured back and forth between them. She made another wild sound and clutched at him, the movement welding their bodies together like two halves of a whole, and he nearly lost it right then. But the taste of tears cut through his senses, and he dragged his mouth away from hers, his heart pounding like a locomotive in his chest.

He looked down into her face, her eyes luminous and full of emotion. And it was dangerous. There was too much familiarity between them, too much need. He swiped his thumbs underneath her eyes, fighting for every breath.

Inhaling jaggedly, he nestled her head closer, turning his face against her head. "It's okay," he whispered against her hair.

She clutched him tighter, as if she were trying to climb right inside him. There was so much desperation in that one small sound, so much fire; it was like a knife in his chest. Her arms locked around him, she choked out his name; then she moved against him, silently pleading with him, pleading with her body—and any connection he had with reason shattered into a thousand pieces.

The feel of her heat against him was too much, and he turned his head against hers. He caught her around the hips, bringing her roughly against him. He needed this—the heat of her, the weight of her. Her. He needed her.

Bridget made another low sound, and then she inhaled raggedly and pulled herself up against his arousal, her voice breaking on a low sob of relief. "Please, Matt." She moved against him again, and Matt tightened his hold even more, unable to stop as he involuntarily responded. Body to body, heat to heat, and suddenly there was no turning back.

Shifting her head, he covered her mouth in a hot, deep kiss, and she opened to him, her mouth moving against his with an urgent hunger. It was too much—and not nearly enough, and Matt caught her behind the knee, dragging her leg around his hip. With one twisting motion, his hard heat was flush against hers. Grasping her buttocks, he thrust against her as she moved with him, riding him, riding the hard thick ridge jammed against her. But that wasn't enough, either. Matt nearly went ballistic, certain he would explode if he didn't get inside her.

Making incoherent sounds against his mouth, Bridget twisted free, and a violent shudder coursed through Matt when he felt her hands fumble with the button and zipper of his pants. The instant she touched his hard throbbing flesh, he groaned out her name and let go of her, desperate to be rid of his clothes.

Bridget unfastened, yanked and pulled until he was naked. The instant he felt her hand close around him, he lost it completely. Jerking her hand away, he backed her onto the chaise. He clenched his eyes shut and thrust into her, unable to hold back one second longer. The feel of her, tight and wet, closing around him drove the air right out of him, the sensation so intense he couldn't move.

Bridget sobbed out his name and locked her legs around him, her movements urging him on. Matt could only feel the white-hot desire rolling over him. Angling his arm across her back, he drove into her again and again, pressure building and building. A low guttural sound was torn from him and his release came in a blinding rush that went on and on, so powerful he felt as if he were being turned inside out. He wanted to let it take him under, but he forced himself to keep moving in her, knowing she was on the very edge. She cried out and clutched at his back, then went rigid in his arms, and she finally convulsed around him, the gripping spasms wringing him dry.

His heart hammering, his breathing so labored he felt almost dizzy, he weakly rested his head against hers, his whole body quivering. He felt as if he had been wrenched in two.

He didn't know how long he lay there, with her trembling in his arms, not an ounce of strength left in him.

It wasn't until she shifted his hold and tucked his

face against hers that he realized her cheek was wet with tears. Hauling in an unstable breath, he turned his head and kissed her on the neck, a feeling of overwhelming protectiveness rising up in his chest. There was no way he could let her go. Not yet. He waited a moment for the knot of emotion to ease, and then he smoothed his hand up her arm to her shoulder.

He levered himself off her and silently they dressed. Neither of them uttered a word on the way back to his house. And when they got there, he opened the passenger door and she looked up at him. He reached out his hand, so seriously needing to be alone and so desperately wanting to bask in Bridget. His love for her won out, thinking now that their time together was finite. He knew it. She knew it.

Just inside his front door, she wrapped her arms around him. Hit with a rush of emotion, Matt nestled her tighter and closed his eyes, slipping his hand across the exposed skin of her back.

Struggling with a thickness in his chest, he began stroking her back, feelings he didn't want to acknowledge crowding in on him. Sliding his hand higher, he rubbed the back of her neck, and he felt her swallow, then swallow again, and he realized she was struggling with some very raw emotions as well. His own throat closed up a little.

Feeling a little raw himself, he cupped his hand along her jaw, and then applied pressure with his thumb to get her to lift her head. Inhaling unevenly, he covered her mouth with a soft, searching kiss, trying to give her some consolation. He knew by how still she went that she was not expecting that, and Matt experienced a flicker of anger. It was almost as if she expected him to push her away and storm off to be alone.

Determined to show her that tonight was special to him, he tightened his hold on her jaw, his tone commanding as he whispered against her mouth. "Open up for me."

Her breath caught, but she yielded to the pressure of his thumb, and Matt adjusted the alignment of his mouth against hers, deepening the kiss with slow, lazy thoroughness. Working his mouth softly, slowly against hers, he drank from her, probing the moist recesses, savoring the taste of her. Her breath caught again, then she finally responded, and he grasped the back of her head, her hair tangling like silk around his fingers. His chest tightening, he massaged the small of her back, and he felt her muscles go slack, as if he had released the rigid tension inside her.

Slipping her arm around him, she mimicked his caress, and Matt let his breath go in a rush, an electrifying weakness radiating through his lower body. She did it again, and he tightened his hold on her hair, feeling himself grow hard.

Dragging his mouth away from her, he gathered her in his arms and marched to the stairs, up to his bedroom.

Laying her down on the bed, he stripped off his clothes and removed hers. Settling her under the covers, he climbed in beside her and brought her back into his arms.

He kissed her ear, tracing the shape with the tip of his tongue, and then trailed his mouth down her neck. Her breathing grew ragged and uneven, and he found her beaded nipple and rubbed his thumb over the taut peak.

She cried out, and she caught his hand, pressing it hard against her breast, until Matt could feel the frantic beat of her pulse beneath his palm. His own breathing suddenly ragged, he caught her around the hips and rolled, drawing her under him. Shifting his weight on his elbows, he then took her face between his hands, holding her head as he kissed her with a thoroughness that made his own heart stammer. Damn, he wanted her.

He flexed his hips, and she rose up to meet him, tightened her muscles around him, and his mind clouded with desire. He would likely go to his grave still wanting her.

MOONLIGHT CAST long, faint shadows through the window, and off in the distance, a lone siren blared.

Bridget glanced up at the man asleep beside her, a disquieting feeling settling low in her stomach. She was lying with her head on his shoulder and her arm around his chest, the rhythm of his breathing indicating a very deep and heavy sleep.

The feelings that rushed through her disturbed her. She tightened her arm around him to keep him close, and then stared at the telescope sitting in front of his balcony.

She stared at it knowing that, although she was

very fond of Matt, their relationship wasn't going to work. He wanted to observe the world at a distance. Stare at it until it made sense, but Bridget wanted to be immersed in the world, a part of it, a player. She wanted to be recognized and praised for her accomplishments. She wanted awards and money and fame.

She thrived on chaos and Matt was overwhelmed by it.

She had embarrassed him tonight and she felt so sorry for it. She hadn't thought it through. The heady feeling of posing naked, the power and beauty of a body she saw no reason to hide bothered him.

His independence was gleaned from silence and deep thought, working in his lab isolated from people and noise. She, on the other hand, found her independence in expressing herself, giving herself truly body and soul to the moment and wringing everything out of it.

They were polar opposites.

Feeling sick at heart and knowing in her soul that once she left Cambridge she would have to leave Matt behind, she pulled away from him. Slipping out of bed, she picked up her dress and underthings and dressed quickly.

Downstairs, she let herself out of Matt's house. Just as silently, she let herself into her aunt's.

"Bridget? Is that you?"

Bridget froze at the front door, her aunt's voice coming from the kitchen.

"Yes. It's me," she responded.

Setting her sandals on the stairs, she entered the kitchen to find her aunt sipping hot chocolate and working a crossword puzzle.

"You're up late?"

"What time is it?"

"About midnight."

"Good grief, is it? Did you have a wonderful time?"

"It was wonderful. Sheila Bowden sketched me. She plans to use my form in a series of charcoal drawings."

"The consummate model, huh?"

"I guess. I like the attention."

"You were always a demanding little girl. Whenever you went off the diving board, you always yelled, 'Watch me, Aunt Ida. Watch me.'"

Bridget laughed. "That's me, the ham."

"If you really did have such a wonderful time, why do you look so sad?"

"It's Matt. We're…um…dating."

"And that makes you sad."

"No, Matt's great. It's just that we don't quite see eye to eye on certain things like posing naked. He wasn't too thrilled."

"He's always been a quiet, mysterious person. Not surprising. His mother was always hovering over him as if she thought he would break."

"Matt's tougher than anyone would ever think."

"How about you, sweetheart. How are things? Really?"

Bridget pasted a smile on her face and answered automatically, "They're fine. I'm moving forward with my plans to market Matt's fabric. Soon he'll be established and I can get back to New York."

"I'll be sorry to see you go. Don't make it so long between visits, huh?"

"I won't."

"What will happen with Matt's business, once you've gone back to New York?"

Bridget looked at her aunt. "What?"

"When you go, who will run the business?"

"I don't know. I really didn't think about it."

"I guess you should think about it." Her aunt turned back to her crossword puzzle. "Good night, Bridget."

"Good night, Aunt Ida."

BRIDGET THREW HERSELF into Matt's business, calling designers, making more garments out of the fabric, mostly to keep her mind busy. Time ebbed and flowed. Monday came and went and the week flew by. It was soon Saturday and time for her mother's garden party.

She hadn't had a chance to see Matt. Their busy schedules didn't mesh. Maybe he decided he didn't want to go, after all. She should ask just to make sure.

She walked over to his house, breathing a sigh of relief when she saw his car in the driveway. Her mouth dry, she knocked on the door. How ridiculous she was being, but she wanted to see him, hear his sexy voice. He didn't come to the door, and Bridget twisted the knob, finding the door unlocked.

He was probably immersed in something and had

tuned everything else out. She wouldn't bother him, but she needed an answer. Who was she kidding? She wanted to see him.

She pushed the door open and called out, "Matt!"

"Upstairs," he replied.

He sounded sexy and distracted. "Hey, I hope I'm not bothering you."

"You're not. Come up."

When she reached his room, he was sitting in the big chair by the window, a sheaf of papers in his hand and his laptop on his knee.

"You look busy."

"I was just finishing up an article for a journal submission. No biggie."

She took a deep breath, feeling as if she was asking the cool guy to the prom. "Good. I was wondering if you still wanted to go to the garden party today. I will understand…"

He set the papers down. "And leave you to the mercy of your mother." He shook his head. "No way. I'm going. Besides I bet they have good food there and I'm starving. I didn't have any breakfast."

"Oh, I'm so glad."

"Bridget?" His voice got rough.

Bridget braced herself, not sure why. "Yes."

He looked down at the computer and swallowed. "Have you stayed away because you wanted to or because you think I need space?"

She moved forward as he closed the laptop and set it beside the chair. Now that she was closer, she saw the lines of tension around his eyes, the corners of his mouth. Funny how quickly she'd learned his face, how easily she spotted even the tiniest difference. "I think you need space."

"Space is for astronauts. I miss you."

"Oh Matt," she said, reaching out and taking his hand in hers. He looked away from her.

"No. It's true." When he shifted his gaze back to hers, the only word she could come up with to describe his expression was...lost. "I know you're going back to New York, but you're here now."

"Yes," she smiled.

"So let's not waste time, okay?"

Her smile dimmed a little as she stroked her fingertips over the back of his hand, surprised at how deeply she felt the need to touch him, reach him. "All right, but you'll let me know if I'm messing up your schedule."

He smiled then and relaxed a little. "To hell with my schedule."

She sat back. "I'm just a big mess maker, aren't I?"

He tugged her forward, then kept on tugging until she stumbled and fell into his lap. "Yes, you are and distracting and beautiful and sweet and complicated." He easily arranged her sideways and lifted her arms around his neck.

"I like being messy." She ran her fingers along the side of his face and he turned into her touch, pressed his lips into the palm of her hand, then cupped her face and pulled her into a kiss.

Considering his mood, she'd expected something needy, slow, exploratory. Instead it was fierce, hard, consuming. It took her breath away and the rest of her conscious thoughts followed. And when she thought he couldn't take any more, he plundered deeper, demanded more. And she gave without question. His hands moved over her body. Her hands did some exploring of their own.

When he finally tore his mouth from hers, her shirt was half-undone and his hair was a tousled mess. He said nothing, just pressed his forehead to her cheek as he held her close while their breathing steadied. She stroked his hair, his neck, his back, collected herself as well, even as her thoughts raced ahead.

In the short time they'd been together, she felt like she'd really come to know him. Understand him. And yet this was a part of him she hadn't expected. Something deeper, more emotional, more...complicated.

When she would have leaned back to look in his eyes, he held her in place, kept her tucked against him. He turned his face so he could nuzzle her hair. "I'm beginning to like messy, too," he said with surprising emotion.

"But it's not something you're accustomed to."

"No." He pulled in a deep breath, and then let it out slowly. "I'm used to caution. Thinking things through. My parents never expected to have children. So, when I came along, they worried about everything. My mother was overly protective. Unfortunately, nothing was mine alone. My parents had to know where I was, what I was doing, what I was getting into, everything. I retreated inwardly, protected myself. You've been the only person I've let get this close to me." He took a deep breath. "That's why Emily and I didn't last. I wouldn't open up to her and she hated it."

"Why is it different with me?"

"It just is. Like I said, you have this way about you that just gets past my defenses. I can't explain it."

"I feel the same way about you, too. We're shaped by the people around us," she murmured, thinking about her mother, the pressure to always make her happy. Her priorities had been ingrained into Bridget. "My mother can be difficult, but she pushed me to succeed which I guess could be a double-edged sword. Everything I did was about the pageants until I lived, breathed and ate them." She lifted her shoulder. "That way of life became my way of life."

She stroked his face, and then lifted his chin until their eyes met. "But we'll always have this connection between us."

He nodded then shifted to look at his watch. "That party's in an hour, so I guess we'd better get ready. If you're late, she'll blame it on me."

Bridget grinned and nodded. "Can I drive the coupe?"

"What? Didn't you just tell me you were messy? I'm not sure it's a good idea to let you drive."

She made a face. "Right, messy, not reckless."

He tugged her down, his kiss slow this time, and exploratory. She relaxed against him, and wondered if she'd ever get tired of this, of him. She didn't think so. A shame they were so suited for each other this way, and not in any other way. If only they'd met under other circumstances.

This way leads to insanity, Bridget. And she couldn't deny that, given half a chance, she'd start trying to figure out some way to mesh his stoic lifestyle with her need for the limelight. Her real life didn't fit with him, though. Reuniting with Matt had been good for her in a lot of really wonderful ways that only began with the best sex she was ever likely to have. Better for her sanity to just shut up, and enjoy it while it lasted. Beat the hell out of never having it in the first place.

Matt ended the kiss on a sigh. "Hmm. Reckless and messy seem the same to me."

Bridget shifted in his lap. "Come on, Matt. Pretty please."

"I can't resist you."

BRIDGET WALKED BACK over to her house, lucky to get out of Matt's house with only tousled hair and a shirt she had to tuck back in. If she was late for her mother's shindig, there would be hell to pay.

The phone was ringing as she opened the front door.

It was Naomi.

"The Web site I set up got some hits but, all in all, there has been a dismal return on our investment and we'll have to come up with a better plan."

"Right. You know, Naomi, I need someone to take over this business once I get it on its feet. You see, I never planned to actually run it. I was hoping you'd be interested."

For a moment Naomi was silent. "You're kidding, right?"

"No. I'm dead serious."

Naomi squealed. "I would love to take over. I love the fabric and I have so many plans. The fabric you ordered is going to be ready soon. We'll have to find a place to store it."

"We'll figure it all out." It was discouraging that the swatch campaign didn't work. She'd have to put her mind to something else.

Naomi disconnected and Bridget went up to her room to get dressed. Feeling suddenly sad, she tried to identify why.

She sat down to freshen her makeup, but found that her eyes started to tear up. Blinking the crazy tears away, she dabbed at them with a tissue.

This was a silly display. She had to go back to New York. She had to make it there. Anything else would be a straight-out failure.

She shook her head. She was feeling blue because she would be able to go back to New York any day now. The business was progressing, in spite of the swatches, and her bank account was now quite hefty with the generous salary Matt paid her. She'd miss Naomi and Aunt Ida.

She'd miss Matt.

God, how she would miss him.

11

BRIDGET STARED at the house that she'd grown up in, the rush of driving Matt's Porsche through Cambridge and up the oak-lined driveway fading.

Built in 1894 the house sat overlooking the Charles River with a fantastic view of the Boston skyline in the winter when the leaves were off the trees. The name River House was lettered in black over the door and obviously came from the spectacular view of the river. The brick walkway leading up to the house was framed by oak trees and flanked by lawns. Bridget couldn't see it, but she remembered the beautiful private garden, accessible from several locations in the home. Enclosed by fencing, surrounded by a bluestone patio and lovely plantings, including rhododendron, azalea, Japanese maple and holly, with the added heated pool centerpiece, the house was made for garden parties.

She'd walked those gardens for the sheer beauty of the blossoms and the fragrance, feeling everything melt away.

The Colonial Revival residence, with its distinctive bowfront facade, was one of the grand houses in the neighborhood. Her mother wouldn't have it any other way. A showpiece of a house was very important to her, unlike her father, who cared more about teaching his students at Harvard, unaffected by his inherited wealth and his social-climbing wife. The three-story residence, which had been carefully renovated by her mother, featured spacious rooms, high ceilings. Each principal room featured a fireplace, adding up to a mind-boggling fourteen, with approximately eleven thousand square feet of living space for two people.

She took Matt's hand and started up the brick path. As they stepped into the grand foyer, her mother walked out of the reception hall where Bridget could see many people bellied up to the wet bar.

"There you are, Bridget. What a lovely dress you're wearing. Is it from Paris?"

Bridget smoothed down the mesh overskirt sewn with her big flowers in rich pastel hues from baby blue to deep blue. The bodice and underskirt was made from a vibrant blueberry dupioni silk. "No. I…made it."

"Did you?" Her mother frowned and gave Matt an unfriendly look. "From his fabric?"

"Just the overskirt. The rest is dupioni silk. I'm just trying different patterns and uses for the fabric."

"I see." Disapproval showed in every line of her face. "Well come in and mingle. Everyone is here, including the mayor's wife."

As they walked through the living room to the doors leading to the rear gardens, Matt whispered, "If looks could kill…"

Bridget giggled and nodded.

"The dress is stunning by the way."

She turned to look at him. "Thanks, charmer."

He grinned, but it soon faded. "Emily."

Bridget turned to find Matt's ex-wife. The woman was as impeccably dressed as she had been that day at Matt's.

"Matt." She looked expectantly at Bridget and her forehead creased. "Do I know you from somewhere?"

"Bridget's a model," Matt said bluntly.

"Oh, that must be it. Emily Wadsworth, Matt's ex-wife."

"Bridget Cole, Matt's lover."

For a moment there was utter silence and then Emily laughed. "You've gotten yourself a live one here. That surprises me. It was a pleasure to meet you. Gorgeous dress."

Something about her expression set off alarm bells in Bridget's head.

Emily moved on in the crowd and Bridget turned to watch her go.

"Bridget, do you have to be so blatant?"

"She started it."

"What do you mean?"

"She acted all possessive. I didn't like it."

"Possessive? She and I are divorced and we've moved on with our lives."

"You might have, but I'm not so sure about her. A woman can sense these things, trust me."

"You have nothing to worry about. I'm going to get a drink at the bar. Do you want anything?"

"A Cosmopolitan, please. Make it a double."

MATT THOUGHT HE WOULD explode with the amount of pent-up energy that seemed to have been building since the night he'd watched an artist sketch Bridget's beautiful body.

"Scotch, straight up and a Cosmopolitan, make it a double, if you can."

"I can guess which one is for you."

He turned at Emily's voice. "I need a drink."

"Parties always did tax your social skills or is it the beautiful Bridget?"

"It's none of your business, Emily."

"That was the problem with our marriage, Matt. Nothing about you was my business. But I didn't come over here to discuss our failed relationship. I'm worried about you."

The bartender set the amber liquid down in a heavy cut-crystal glass next to the elegant Cosmo. Matt picked up the Scotch and downed its contents. "Why would you be worried about me?"

"Bridget seems like a nice person, but I bet she's also very ambitious. I don't think she'll be amenable to being slotted into your life. Don't think for a moment that I didn't recognize her from that *On* article. She's no more a CEO than I'm a bimbo. You're the smarts behind that facade. God forbid you should be exposed in any way."

Matt narrowed his eyes. "Look, Emily, I'm a big boy and I can take care of myself. Thanks for your concern, but it's unwarranted."

"Is it? I think probably this was the woman that was always between us. I think you've always been in love with her. A woman like that naturally brings notice. Watch out, Matt, she'll bring your world crashing down."

His mouth went dry. Damn women and their ability to see things so clearly. His gut clenched, hard. He'd had a week to contemplate what life would be like without Bridget. He felt almost desperately giddy when she'd checked to make sure he was still going with her to the Garden Party.

A long week. He resented the need even as he felt it. He wasn't the kind of man to have fanciful notions and romantic needs, but with Bridget all his carefully crafted thoughts seemed to dry up and blow away, so much ash.

His work had always sustained him. If he had to examine his feelings for Bridget, it would take him a century. All tied up in knots and teetering on the edge of madness, he picked up the Cosmo and headed through her mother's ostentatious house to find the woman who was driving him to complete and utter distraction.

As for Emily's dire warning, Matt just couldn't be that concerned about MIT finding out that he was the brains behind the sexy lingerie fabric. A disaster to be sure, but it was the thought of losing Bridget to a life that caused her so much anxiety, a life that he just couldn't imagine himself fitting into that really worried him.

Yet he wanted her in his life. The need to tell her…everything pressed against his brain and his heart.

"Excuse me?"

Bridget turned away from the conversation that she'd been embroiled in for the last ten minutes by two of her mother's dearest friends, who were pumping her for information about the latest fashions from Paris. An elegantly dressed woman waited expectantly to catch her attention.

Bridget kept her society smile in place. "Yes," she answered, steering the woman away from her mother's friends, who closed ranks and continued to talk.

"I'm sorry to bother you, but I just had to know where you got that dress."

"I made it, actually."

"Did you really? I own Clarice's Unique Boutique downtown." She stuck out her hand. "Clarice Wentworth."

Bridget took it and shook. "Bridget Cole."

"It's a pleasure to meet you. I would love one in each size if you could manage it."

"I don't know. I don't really..." The woman looked so eager Bridget couldn't say no. "All right."

"Wonderful. Here's my card. Please call me when they're ready and tell me what you'd charge for each."

Bridget took the card and smiled. "Charge? Right. Charge. I'll call tomorrow."

"Wonderful. My young clients are going to fight over these dresses."

"I told you that your designs were to die for, honey."

Bridget's head jerked up at the sound of Danny's voice, but her greeting died in her throat. Danny was dressed in a lavender and yellow summer dress with a short knit sweater in a lemon-yellow. He had a large straw sun hat on his head with violet sprigs gracing the brim. With his face made up and his long dark hair out of the ponytail he usually wore, he looked stunning.

Reaching out, he put his finger beneath her chin and closed her mouth. "Speechless?"

"To say the least. What are you doing here?"

"I'm a member of your mother's society club."

Bridget covered her mouth with her hand.

"Isn't it delicious? She doesn't even suspect a thing."

"How long have you been a member?"

"About six months. So Clarice wants to buy your dress. How does that feel?"

"Crazy, since I've never considered my sewing worth cold hard cash. I didn't go to school for designing."

"You have natural talent. Who's to say you're not a designer. If someone wants the goods, you deliver, sister. You ever need anything from the BQU, you let us know. We're here for you. Ta ta."

With a wave, he moved across the lawn with a sexy hip swing. She really would have to catch his show in Boston. He was something else.

"Hey there," Matt said, and she turned around to find him holding the Cosmopolitan. He handed it to her and she took it, taking a sip.

"Thanks, I needed this."

"Tough crowd?"

"You have no idea."

He took her hand and led her toward some box hedges that shielded them from the other guests. "Matt, what are you doing?"

"I need to talk to you."

"Okay." She sipped her Cosmo, met his eyes and everything inside her froze. She fell into his intense eyes and her heart did a slow barrel roll in her chest.

"Matt don't…"

"There you are," her mother said. "I've been looking all over for you. You need to attend to your social obligations. Come now. I'd like to introduce you to Sylvia Moore. She's dying to know all about your life in New York."

Dragging Bridget away from Matt, the rest of her Cosmopolitan sloshed out of the glass. Bridget mourned its loss.

"Wait a damn minute."

Bridget had never heard Matt use that tone of voice. It seemed to come from some tortured place inside him.

Experiencing a flurry of emotions, Bridget tried to get her mother to release her, but the woman had a death grip on her wrist.

Finally, her mother stopped in the middle of the lawn, Matt close on her heels. "What is it? Can't it wait?"

"No. It can't wait. Damn, but you are a selfish woman. Don't you understand anything? I want to talk to your daughter in private."

"What could you possibly have to say that is so important?"

"I love her, dammit!"

His loud proclamation carried across the lawn and everyone within shouting distance turned their heads. Some smiled, others nodded, the silence deafening.

Her mother dropped her wrist and looked at him with horror. Feeling suddenly shaky inside, Bridget met his eyes. "What did you just say?"

"I love you. It's not exactly the way I wanted to tell you, but I can't hold it back any longer."

Bridget grabbed his wrist and dragged him from the lawn, up the stairs of the patio and through the French doors into the living room. Thinking frantically where they could go in her mother's overrun house, the answer came to her.

She dragged him into the library, closing the ornate mahogany doors firmly behind her. Her insides a tangle of uncertainty, she pulled him into the English greenhouse and stood there staring.

Her chest filled up with all kinds of emotions too overwhelming to define and suddenly her vision blurred. God, but she loved him.

A confused frown appeared on Matt's forehead. "Bridget?"

She tried to smile as she stroked his cheek with her thumb, wonder unfolding in her.

She stared at him for an instant longer, and then she closed her eyes and came into his arms, holding on to him with a desperate strength. Matt turned his face against her neck, locking his arms around her.

"I think I've loved you forever," he whispered, his breath sending chills across her skin. Stepping away, he cupped her chin and turned her face up to his. "I don't have a childhood memory without you in it. These last weeks have been great." He slid his hand under her hair and caressed her neck.

Inhaling raggedly, the air perfumed with flowers, she tightened her hold on him, an agony of relief rushing through her. She released a soft sob.

He leaned down and brushed her lips with a soft, undemanding kiss. Bridget closed her eyes and opened her mouth beneath his, not wanting to let go of him ever, not sure if she could make good on that desire. Matt held her head still as he deepened the kiss, his mouth moist and warm as he leisurely worked it back and forth against hers. She grasped his arm to steady herself, a tingling weakness traveling from the top of her head to the tips of her toes. Sliding his fingers into her hair, he increased the pressure, and the kiss turned deep and carnal.

Releasing a shaky sigh, Matt eased away, then swore softly and gathered her up in a snug, comforting embrace. Rubbing his jaw along the top of her head, he locked his arms around her hips. "Bridget, please say something. I'm dying here."

Bridget slid her arms around his neck. "I love you, too."

"Thank God," he whispered raggedly. Brushing his mouth softly against hers, he felt something change, escalate into something more.

Feeling almost desperate, she tightened her arms around his neck. "Oh, Matt…"

Her face wet with tears, she cradled his head with both arms, unbearable tenderness filling her to the very brim. God, but she loved him. Right down to her soul.

Matt didn't move for the longest time, and then he exhaled with a shudder and shifted his hold. "I'm going to have to sit down," he whispered unevenly. "Just don't let go."

Bridget couldn't have let go if her life depended on it, and she nodded and stroked the back of his head. Tightening his grip around her, he turned using a table full of gardenias as a back brace as he lowered them both to the ground.

The greenhouse floor was tiled, and cold on Bridget's legs as she tucked them back, straddling his hips. Still cradling his head against her breast, she pressed a soft kiss against his hair, the dim light inside the greenhouse making her even more acutely aware of him.

Running his hands up her arms, he turned his head and kissed her just under her ear, then spoke, a faint trace of amusement in his voice, "This is the very first time in my life that I've ever drawn attention to myself like that. It's your fault."

Smiling, Bridget bracketed his face with her hands, resting her forehead against his. "No, it most certainly isn't my fault."

He chuckled. "Whose fault is it?"

"My mother's."

At the surprised look on his face, she laughed, sliding her arms around his neck.

"You're right. If she'd only given me some privacy." She felt him smile, and he tightened his hold and gave her a firm hug. "Then again, we might never have said what we said."

"You're an opportunist, Fox."

"Open the henhouse and I'm there, baby. I never turn down a plump chicken."

She laughed against his face, hugging him back hard.

"We'd better go," he murmured, his voice soft. "With our luck, your mother will come out here on the pretense of picking up an orchid."

Hooking his thumb under her chin, he angled her head, giving her a soft, sweet kiss, and then he released another sigh. Grasping her by the waist, he supported her as she eased off him. The dimness affected her sense of balance, and Matt held her arm until she steadied herself, then he got up, brushing against her. "It's my new favorite fragrance."

He left the greenhouse and Bridget followed, clamping her hand across her mouth to stifle her mirth until she got it under control.

"Geez, woman," he whispered, his voice quivering with his own suppressed laughter. "Be quiet. I don't know about you, but I've made enough of a spectacle of myself for one day."

Fighting to contain herself, she nodded, her shoulders starting to shake. Matt put his finger to his lips as he eased the library door open. Miraculously, no one was there.

"Where did everyone go?"

"They're probably at the lecture."

"What lecture?"

"My mother has a speaker come for almost all her functions."

"What's the topic?"

"Dirt, I think."

That started off another round of giggles. "Damn," Matt said jumping away from the door and closing it. "Everyone's coming back in. We can't get out that way."

"How about we go through the greenhouse?"

"Sounds like a plan."

Except when they got to the outside door, it was padlocked.

Bridget swore under her breath and looked around. She saw the window at the same time Matt did. Bridget shook her head, held her hands up and backed away, nearly overcome by a fit of silent giggles. If he thought she was going to climb through that window—in a dress—he was out of his mind.

Giving her a sidelong glance, he grinned. "Piece of cake."

She shook her head again, but he totally ignored her. Grasping the ledge, he hoisted himself up and popped out the screen, then jumped down, dusting his hands off on the seat of his now-dirty pants. Turning to her, he grinned and locked his hands together, a clear indication he wanted to boost her up.

"You would want me to go first."

"Hey, I can get up there by myself. You, on the other hand, need help."

"Oh, all right." She pulled off her sandals, grumbling. She stepped on his cupped hands and he thrust her up to the windowsill. She grasped the ledge, bracing her chest and pulling herself up and over the sill, dropping down onto the ground below.

Matt soon followed. They hightailed it for Matt's Porsche, laughing like schoolchildren who'd just gotten away with a silly prank on the stern principal.

Once in the car, stifling another fit of laughter, she slid her arm around him and turned her face into his damp neck. "My hero."

She felt him smile. "Heroes get good perks." He brushed her hair back with both hands, then, tightening his hold on her face, leaned down and kissed her, his mouth warm and moist and unbearably tender. Bridget experienced a rush of emotion so intense that it made her lungs clog up. Suddenly the laughter was gone, replaced by something very painful. She wondered how long it would be before the bubble would burst and reality would sweep in. When would all this magic disappear from her life forever?

Tightening his hold on her face, Matt released his breath and drew away. His expression sober, he stared down at her, the sun shining brightly on his hair. His eyes fixed on hers, he said quietly, "What's up, Bridget?"

Trying to smile, she shook her head. "Nothing."

He pressed his thumb against her mouth, his gaze unwavering, as if he was assessing her. There wasn't a trace of amusement in his voice when he spoke again. "It'll work out."

There was something in his tone that made her heart roll over, and for a minute, she was afraid her eyes were going to fill up. She nodded. "It will," she whispered.

His expression very somber, he drew his thumb across her bottom lip, then he met her gaze again. "This isn't some game I'm playing, Bridget."

"I know," she whispered.

He continued to watch her, his expression still thoughtful, then he spoke. "It'll work out. It has to."

Feeling as if he'd pulled the ground out from under her, she stared at him. It was as if he'd peeled away some protective layer, leaving her without any defenses, and blood rushed to her ears.

He stared a second longer, then gave her a small twisted smile and put the car in gear.

She closed her eyes; the only words that came to her were, *If it's too good to be true...*

12

HIS WHOLE BODY trembling, Matt clenched his jaw, his heart still slamming in his chest, the intensity of his release leaving him totally spent. It was the sense of smell that returned to him first. The musky scent of sex, sweat and hot skin. And the feel of her tight around him, gripping him, anchoring him deep inside her. It felt so good. So damned good.

Drained dry by the thick, wringing climax, Matt inhaled unevenly and turned his face against her sweat-dampened neck, the rush of blood still pounding through his head. He lay unmoving until his pulse rate quieted, then he stirred, his body heavy, his muscles slow to respond. Dredging up what little strength he had left, he braced his weight on his forearms, his chest contracting when he realized how desperately Bridget was hanging on to him.

Sensation wrenched loose in his chest, and he closed his eyes and rested his head against hers, his throat suddenly contracting.

Not wanting to think, he drenched his senses with the heated scent of her, trying not to think at all.

Finally getting it together, he inhaled unevenly and lifted his head. Murmuring her name, he reached behind him, loosening her hold around his back, and then pressing her down against the bed. She lay with her eyes clenched shut, and he could feel her trembling beneath him. Smoothing her damp hair back from her face, he leaned down and softly kissed her mouth, then lifted his head and gazed down at her. "Bridget?"

She drew a deep, sated breath, and then opened her eyes. Matt felt his expression soften as he caressed the line of her jaw.

"Don't even think about asking me to move," she warned.

He laughed. "Not even for sustenance as in 'I'm starving and if you want any more mind-blowing sex, I need to get me some food.'"

"Food," she breathed softly, opening one blue eye. "As long as I don't have to move."

"I don't think food is going to make itself," he said, tweaking her nose. Her response was to slap his hand away.

She rolled her eyes. "Sure it is. It's called takeout." This time she opened both eyes and gave him a cheeky smirk.

He grinned stupidly, getting lost in her sleepy gaze. "Takeout."

"You know." She pantomimed picking up the phone and dialing. "You use the phone, talk into it and food appears like magic on your doorstep," she said with a laugh. "Simple."

He grinned and rolled off her. "Okay, smarty-pants. What do you want?"

"Chinese would be heavenly—egg roll, chicken fried rice, crab Rangoon and egg drop soup."

"Yowza, someone is hungry."

"Your fault. You have had your way with me since we got back from the garden party—" she raised herself on her elbow and looked at the clock "—four hours ago. Now get on that phone and order us some food. I'm eating for two."

"Huh?"

She chuckled. "That's what I say as a joke." She moved and slapped her butt. "You know," she said, pointing to the globes of her ass. "One and two."

"Right, a joke from the sleeping woman," he said, striving to keep it light, because suddenly it all felt a bit too earth-shattering and very terrifying, so he figured she was feeling the same way and wanted to change the subject.

"Hey, I'm awake enough to know that you haven't picked up that phone."

"Bitch, bitch, nag, nag," he grumbled with a smile and snatched up his bedside phone. He quickly placed the order, feeling the bed move. Setting the receiver in the cradle, he crowed while hunching back into the pillows. "She's alive!"

Bridget's response was to growl and throw a pillow at him.

He watched her naked form cross his bedroom, appreciating the rear view, watching the lazy, loose-hipped way she moved. After a few minutes, Matt called out. "It's pretty quiet in there."

She materialized in the doorway. "You bought me a toothbrush."

"You were contemplating the toothbrush purchase?"

"It's just that it's so sweet and thoughtful that you would care enough to make me comfortable while I'm here."

"I do want you to feel comfortable."

She came out of the bathroom and went to slip back into bed, but someone knocked at the door.

Grabbing up Matt's dress shirt, she shoved her arms into the sleeves and buttoned it up. "I'll get that. You stay here." Taking her purse, she dashed out the door.

Matt thought he was going to be hard-pressed to keep up with her and he got out of bed, grabbed a pair of shorts and a T-shirt and went downstairs.

Bridget was just finishing up with the purchase and she brought the brown paper sack toward him. "Hey, let's have a picnic in the living room."

Matt pulled pillows from the couch and lined them up against the edge of the fireplace. Bridget served up the food onto plates, poured the soup into mugs and brought it over. They settled down to eat.

"It's too bad it's too warm for a fire." Bridget forked up a bite of chicken and rice and chewed.

Matt nodded. "My parents liked to have a fire every night in the winter. I used to fall asleep to the smell of wood smoke. That smell always makes me think of home." Matt took a sip of the egg drop soup, savoring the rich broth.

"You are the most grounded person I know and you're so content with that."

Matt shrugged. "You make that sound like it's a bad thing."

"It's not. I can't sit still long enough to know if I would like it. I like being on the go."

"You would have to like that lifestyle to do what you do."

Bridget moved closer to him, her bare thigh rubbing over his. Enticed, he enjoyed the tactile stimulation. She cupped the back of his neck and kneaded.

"We're opposites, Matt. We just have a great time together."

"I know." He shifted fully against Bridget, giving her a faint smile. "We have to find a middle ground."

Bridget picked up an egg roll, dipped it into duck sauce and offered him a bite. He took it. She dipped it in again and took her own bite. Wiping her mouth on a napkin, she said, "I hope that's possible."

Matt nodded. "I hope so, too."

Silence settled over them. Feeling no need to break the cocoon of tranquility, Matt pulled Bridget into his arms and held her as they drowsed together, his hand stroking along her thigh. Sated, he sighed.

He could see this working out. How peaceful and full their lives could be. He had his teaching and research that would sustain his mind. When he got home, he'd have Bridget to stimulate him body and soul.

Matt broke the silence. "Are you asleep? Do you want to move upstairs?"

"No, I was thinking. Believe me. It's not easy to use your brain after mind-blowing sex and good food."

"Thinking about what?"

"My next step. The swatch campaign isn't working. Designers have such a demand for their time, so that's not really much of a surprise, but I was hoping for a better response."

"Things will work out. I think you need to give it more time."

"I don't really have more time. I need to get back to New York."

"Why do you feel such pressure to be back in the city? Maybe distance from modeling will give you a new perspective on what you really want to do."

She swiveled against him. "What I really want to do? I know what I want to do."

"I'm just saying you could look at your options."

She met his gaze. "I have to go back. Anything else would be admitting defeat. I'm not going out like that."

"You haven't failed. You won the Miss National pageant and worked in the business for twelve years, Bridget. Not many models last past twenty. Have you thought about doing something else with your talents?"

Bridget got up, picking up the empty plates, and moved away from him. "I love modeling—the traveling, the clothes, the limelight. I don't want to give it up for something else." She moved toward the kitchen and put the plates in the sink.

"What about us?"

Matt followed with the glasses and soup bowls, setting them in the sink.

"You're asking me to choose?"

"No. I wouldn't do that, but I don't see how I'll fit into your life, Bridget. When you put yourself into something, you go all the way. You have a demanding lifestyle that requires you to be flexible, travel."

"I can't talk about this right now. Everything with my life is up in the air. I was straightforward with you all the way. I realize that you like to plan everything, but, Matt, sometimes that's not possible. Let's just take every day as it comes." Bridget gathered up the used containers and put everything into the brown paper bag the meal arrived in and dumped it in the garbage.

He took a deep breath. "I do like to plan everything. It's ingrained. I'll try to be patient."

She crossed the room. Cupping her face in her hand, he realized, not for the first time, how readily she was able to look past the surface with him. She smiled despite the concern still coloring her gaze. "That's all I ask," she intoned, the scent of her hair stirring his senses.

He kissed her, mostly because he couldn't be this close and not. But also because he felt a need to seal things between them.

When he finally lifted his head, she traced her fingers over his lips. As her arms came down, she hit her purse with her elbow and knocked it over. It landed with a thud against the wood of the table and a white card fell out, floated down to the floor near his feet.

He bent to pick it up. "What's this?"

Bridget glanced at it as she picked up the items that had spilled onto the table and the floor. "It's a business card from Clarice Wentworth. She owns that boutique downtown. Very upscale. She wants one of my dresses in every size and I couldn't say no. I have to figure out how much to charge, though. This is so new to me."

"It was a smart idea to wear the dress in public, giving every one a sneak peek one-woman fashion show of your own."

"What did you say?"

"Wearing the dress in public…"

"No, the fashion show part. Matt, that's a great idea." She kissed him full on the mouth and in a flash she headed up the stairs. She called out. "You are a genius."

He had to take the stairs two at a time to keep up with her. When he got to his bedroom door, she already had his drawers open. Pulling out a pair of his shorts, she slipped them on. Next she wiggled into one of his T-shirts and bent down to retrieve the sexy sandals and slipped on the spiky heels.

"Bridget? I thought you were going to stay?"

"I can't, not tonight. Sorry, but I pledged to do a job for you. I've got to get to Naomi and figure out how I'm going to pull this off. I need a theme and models and lighting," she mumbled to herself as she gathered up her dress.

She kissed him on the way out the door and then she was gone. It was only moments later that he heard the front door open and close.

She was energy personified and her whole face lit up when she was on the trail of an idea. He had to admire her for taking a concept and running with it. He was pretty sure that Bridget really knew nothing about hard-core business. But he'd bet she could have been quite the marketing executive if she'd wanted to go back to school. In fact, he was sure that Lesley University had a program.

He would mention it to her. Now that he'd found her again, he didn't want to lose her. Going to school would give her options. It would also keep her here in Cambridge and give them a fighting chance at making this relationship work. The solemn moment in the car came back to him and dread tightened his gut.

It had to work out. He wouldn't accept anything less.

BRIDGET'S HEART POUNDED as her heels click-clacked against the pavement. Why hadn't she thought about organizing a fashion show before? Bridget had numerous contacts and New York was only three and a half hours from Cambridge. This could work.

The whole day and evening with Matt had been wonderful, until they'd gotten onto the subject of her going back to New York. She loved him very much, but she could not fail. She wanted to make the decision to leave modeling, not because she had no other choice.

She wouldn't be a little washed-up nobody.

Overwhelmed suddenly with her emotions, she stopped in the middle of the sidewalk, her hand on her abdomen. She turned to look back at Matt's house, such a place of refuge for her, both in her childhood and now. She took a deep breath.

She didn't have time to waffle or let her unpredictable emotions slow her down. She mentally put them in a box and deliberately closed the lid. Now was the time to think and plan to accomplish what she set out to do.

Bridget burst into the house and ran for the phone. Naomi answered right away. Ignoring the knots in her stomach, Bridget smiled and said, "I've got a great idea. Those bolts of fabric will not be sitting in that storage unit we rented for too much longer."

"What's your idea?"

"A fashion show."

Naomi gasped. "Are you crazy? We don't even have enough clothes to show at a fashion show. Where are we going to get models? You're crazy."

Bridget's smile was so wide it strained the corners of her mouth. "No I'm not. I've thought about this and I've got the perfect answer. BQU."

"Oh, my God." Naomi burst out laughing. "You are the cleverest person."

"Let's call an emergency meeting."

They set the meeting for 9:00 a.m. the next morning. The six members of the BQU filed into her aunt Ida's house with Naomi on the speakerphone. After they were seated and refreshments served, Bridget brought up the idea.

"Oh, honey, you will have to let me help you do the sewing. I make all my own costumes and I'm the

perfect person as the dresser and backstage manager.
I have experience."

"We all know that, Danny," Betty Sue called out.

Everyone laughed and the planning got started in earnest.

"What about models?" Naomi asked.

"I think we have that covered. Ladies?" A murmur of agreement and pleasure circled around the room like a wave.

"After all we are Queens with stunning shapes," Betty Sue said with her unique drawl.

"Have you thought about what type of fashion show to stage, Bridget?" Danny asked, reaching for a flaky croissant from a silver serving tray on the coffee table.

"What do you mean?" Lacy Cuthbert, the Mall Queen, asked with a frown. "Isn't there only one kind?"

"No," Bridget said, smiling at the perky blonde. "There are really four different types. The production show involves singing and dancing, not possible for us. There's the formal runway, but I don't think that's the way to go, or, of course, the video, too impersonal. I think the informal show is going to be the best choice. I've already called the Bowden Gallery and talked to Sheila Bowden. She has tons of space at her gallery. It'll get patrons in to look at the art she offers and let us show off our fashions."

"What's an informal show?" Beth Lambert, the African American Queen asked.

"Is it like in the mall where women walk around and show off the clothes?" Lacy asked.

"Bingo," Bridget said. "Sheila said we could set up tables and offer it as a tea. I've already come up with what I think is a great title, but we can debate it if you all don't agree."

"Tell us, Bridget," Danny chided.

"Cheesecake." A lot of head bobbing and smiles all around made Bridget think she had a winner. "Since we're offering mostly lingerie, à la cheesecake, I thought it would be a novel idea to do little round cheesecakes as dessert with a choice of topping. What do you think?"

"It's fabulous, Bridget," Danny said. "What do you mean by mostly lingerie?"

"I want to showcase the fabric in that venue because it's perfect for lingerie, but I also want to show the versatility of the fabric by using it in other fashions. Dresses, blouses, et cetera."

"Gotcha, sister."

Bridget rose and handed out copies of a calendar with deadlines. "Now the time frame. I've found out from a contact in New York that there will be a Fashion Trade Show at the Boston Convention Center starting June 27. That's a Wednesday. I thought we could offer preconvention entertainment."

All the women and Danny looked at each other. "That's a week and a half away. Where's the sewing machine," Danny said. "We'd better get started."

"Wait a second," Bridget said, picking up her planner. "First we have to delegate each job." She distributed another handout to each of the members. "I've come up with a list. Danny, as you said, you have experience with stage management, so I'm putting you in charge of lighting and staging. We need to be mostly concerned with the placement of the tables to make sure the models can get around them easily, since we won't have a formal stage."

"Check."

"Also, you so graciously offered to handle the dressing which I am grateful for. As a model, I know how important timing is."

"Glad to do it, doll. We Queens have to stick together. If you need additional help, my friends from the show would be glad to assist."

"Thanks, Danny." Bridget consulted her sheet. "I'll handle publicity and merchandise." Bridget addressed Naomi. "If you could handle the models and rehearsal, Naomi, that would be great."

"Can do," Naomi said.

"I thought we could all deal with the invitations and selling the tickets."

"Why don't we give them away for free?" Lacy asked.

"Oh no, we never offer anything for free in the fashion world," Bridget responded. "I thought we'd donate what we collect on the tickets to one of Sheila's worthy artists.

"Also, ladies, I've made up cards with all the pertinent information we'll need to make clothing in your size. Please fill it out and if you're not sure, I have a measuring tape."

Bridget concluded, "Ladies, I can't thank you enough for pitching in and helping. I fully expect to compensate you all for your time. I've got applications and…"

"That won't be necessary, Bridget," Betty Sue said, coming to stand next to her, wrapping her arm around her and giving her a squeeze. "The BQU has pledged to help a Queen in need."

How was she ever going to leave these wonderful people when it came time to go back to New York?

Best to keep that emotional box closed, too, and move ahead.

13

"DANNY, I CAN'T THANK YOU enough for all that you've done. These garments have turned out beautiful. It's hard to believe that the show is this afternoon." The days had whirled by as Bridget, Naomi and the BQU got involved in every aspect of the show. Danny came by almost daily, squeezing in the sewing and the fittings.

"Oh, honey, it's my pleasure. But the pieces are lovely because of your design, not my sewing."

Bridget got up from the makeshift table and picked up a gift box on the bed. Her bedroom had turned into a beehive of activity. She'd rented a table and another sewing machine so that she and Danny could work side by side on her designs. "I wanted to give you this for all your help."

"You didn't have to do that, sweetie." He opened the box and pulled out the blouse she'd made for him, the one he'd admired on her the first time they'd met.

"Oh my," he breathed. "It's simply exquisite. Thank you, Bridget."

The look of joy and admiration on his face made Bridget feel wonderful. She looked at all the clothing hanging on a rack up against her bedroom wall and satisfaction whispered over her, settling deep into her soul. She had to admit that nothing in her life compared to this feeling.

"I was thinking, Bridget. I would be happy to sew those dresses you need for Clarice."

"You would?"

"Now that everything is done for the show, I know I'll miss it. I just love to sew."

"I'll have to pay you for it, Danny. I wouldn't feel right about you doing it for free."

"I can live with that, sweetie."

"Good."

Naomi came into the room smiling. "We're sold out. I sold the last ticket ten minutes ago. We have a full house." She high-fived Bridget.

"That's great," Bridget said. "I think Wednesday is a perfect day for an afternoon show. Over the hump day."

Bridget's cell phone rang and she flipped it open.

"Bridget, it's Leslie."

"Leslie. What's up?"

"You are. I got a call from Maggie Winterbourne. She's named you as the model she wants to define her Independent Woman campaign. She's quite impressed with your accomplishments."

Bridget's heart squeezed painfully. Matt. How was he going to take it? She couldn't think about that right now. It was hard enough just dealing with the news that she was going to model again. "I've been hoping for this kind of break for a long time. This is amazing news."

She looked at Danny and Naomi then covered the receiver. "I got the contract with Maggie."

Danny whooped and Naomi grabbed Bridget and hugged her.

"She wants you in New York tomorrow to take care of the preliminaries. There's going to be television spots, runway work and an intensive magazine spread. She wants to start shooting on Monday in Los Angeles to start off. Then after that, there will be Chicago, Atlanta, Dallas and then back to New York. Can you swing that?"

"I sure can. I'm thrilled, Leslie. Thank you."

"It wasn't me, Bridget. She was quite impressed with you the night she met you at Rags. Good going, girl. Looks like you hit the big time. I'll see you tomorrow."

"Bye, Leslie."

She spent the next few minutes basking in her friends' praise, feeling relief that she'd finally gotten what she tried so hard to achieve. Her mother would be so proud.

"Bridget, why don't you take some time off? You look tired. Everything is in place for this afternoon," Naomi suggested, picking up the garments piled on Bridget's table and placing them on the rack.

"I'm fine. I've got a few more things to do."

"No, we can handle it. Why don't you go over and see Matt. Tell him the good news. I think he's feeling neglected."

Her heart competed with her stomach to see which could squeeze more tightly. "He has been neglected.

I've only managed to have a couple of quick dinners with him in the last week."

"Then get."

The preparations had taken a toll. She needed to see Matt desperately. Denying herself the pleasure had been the most difficult part of the fashion show preparation.

When he opened his door, he gave her a big smile. "Hey. You got a break?"

He took her in his arms and kissed her mouth and she sank into his embrace, marveling how his touch could make her melt, make her desperate for more. Suddenly, without warning, her eyes stung.

When he raised his head, she said, "Yes. I did and I wanted to spend it with you."

"Lucky me." He frowned, looking down into her face. "What's wrong?"

"Nothing." Bridget smiled, even as the ache inside her grew.

"Are you sure?" He captured her wrist and pulled her over to the kitchen table. "I wanted to show you something. I picked these up for you."

He handed her glossy brochures and a booklet. "What are these?"

"An application and information from Lesley University. I thought you might be interested in marketing, since you've done such a great job with my business—"

"Matt." She touched his arm. "I got a contract with Maggie Winterbourne. She's a major designer. I'm going back to New York tomorrow. I've already talked to Naomi. She's shifting most of her CPA practice to an associate to work for you. It's her dream job. She loves it and wants to stay."

"And you don't." He looked away. "What about us, Bridget?" he said, his voice cracking.

Her heart was coming apart with every word he spoke. "We can work it out."

He took her by the arms. "How? On weekends? That's not the kind of life I want with you," he said with a quiet calm that belied the storm in his eyes.

"I just need time to see this through." Bridget knew she had to be strong, be rational, not give in to the emotion that swirled inside her.

"Until when? Until you get another contract, or become famous? What do you want me to do? Just forget about you? Wait around for the phone calls, the e-mails?"

"Matt. I don't have the answers right now. I need to take this contract. It's everything I've worked for."

"I love you. Doesn't that mean a thing to you?"

"Yes, it does, but I think we can make this work if you're open-minded about it."

"You want the limelight more than you want me. That's what this is all about."

"I want to make it in the profession I chose. Don't you think I don't know how lopsided this relationship is? You made it. You're a successful professor at MIT with patents and inventions and something real. I want you to think of me as an equal and that's hard to do when you think what I do is meaningless."

"I didn't say what you do is meaningless."

"No. Is that why you picked up college brochures? People go to college to better themselves."

"I wanted you to have options."

She stepped back, staring at him as if she didn't know who he was. "Oh God, my mother was right. You do look down at me from your lofty academic perch. I don't need this. I've got enough of my own fear and doubt, Matt. I don't need you judging me. If you'll excuse me, I have a fashion show to manage." Turning on her heel, she left his house, carefully closing the door behind her.

When she got home, she entered the house and the activity was at an all-time high. Closing her eyes and shoving everything she was feeling into that emotional box she carried around with her, she locked her pain and disillusionment inside.

Rolling up her sleeves, she entered the fray. They had a fashion show to put on and fabric to sell.

That would be her focus and her lifeline to keep her from breaking down completely.

THE AIR WAS FILLED with a fine-tuned anxiety. Bridget peeked out at the audience seated at tables draped with cream damask tablecloths with fresh fruit centerpieces.

The caterer had arrived on time, but had forgotten the toppings. It was a tense thirty minutes while one of her employees ran back to get them.

Everything was in place. Danny had come through with his friends, two funny guys who had all the models laughing to break the tension.

Naomi walked up to her. "The fashion editors are

seated in the front like you asked and we have a full house of buyers, designers, press and excited citizens."

"Great. We're almost ready to begin. Did you see Matt?"

"No, not yet. Are you okay?"

"Matt and I had a major fight and I think we're over."

"I'm sorry."

"It's okay." Bridget turned and hugged her. "You've been great through all this. I couldn't have asked for a better friend. I never knew what I was missing until I met you and the BQU."

"This is a dream job come true, but I'm going to miss working with you."

"I'm going to miss you, period," Bridget said.

Just then soft music filled the air and the conversation died. Waiters started serving the small rounds of cheesecake on fine cream china, while another waiter went around to the served tables to ask which topping the ladies preferred.

Bridget gathered up her commentary and made her way to the small podium set up in the corner of the gallery. She tested the mike to make sure she had sound and breathed a sigh of relief when she heard the telltale microphone noise.

She laid her papers down and turned on the small light. As she stood there waiting for the din of serving to die down, she felt a calm come over her, seep into her bones and make her feel as if somehow she was at home.

It was then she saw him, standing near the front

door dressed in a pair of dark slacks, open-necked shirt and a sport jacket. His hair was tousled as if he'd been running his hands through it. Their gazes met and locked. Bridget felt an overwhelming sense of love followed closely by one of loss. The calm she had achieved shattered into a million pieces and she had to fight to keep her feet in place. She wanted to run to him, fall into his arms and make the world dissolve. But she couldn't do that and their differences in lifestyle, not to mention their dreams, now stood between them.

He smiled at her and she smiled back as he took a seat in the back at the same table as Clarice Wentworth, the shop owner who had ordered dresses Bridget still had to deliver. But thanks to Danny, that was a done deal.

With a shock, she realized that his ex-wife was also sitting at that table, watching their exchange with interest, looking as if she had her own personal agenda. Bridget's stomach knotted and her palms dampened with perspiration.

She took a deep breath as the music changed. Her cue to begin speaking. "Good afternoon and thank you all for coming. You're about to see some naughty unmentionables made from a wonderful new fabric called Almostnaked. Please refer to your program for available colors and ordering information." The lights dimmed.

"This halter baby doll ensemble in delicate floral lace and bold new colors makes a spectacular statement to the man in your life. And you can bet he'll have something to say about the way this sexy piece heats up his night. Available in lemonade, hot pink, flame-red and black."

Two models emerged from the curtained alcove as a collective gasp came from the audience. One woman modeled the piece in lemonade and the other in black. The women took their places under the pot lights among the patrons and posed there for a moment.

"Almostnaked is a versatile product, going from lacy fabric to this piece with corset-inspired lacing up each side to play a sexy game of peek-a-boo with your curves. Daringly low in front, with slim adjustable straps, it comes in ice-blue, naughty pink, ooh-la-la red and basic black."

Another two of the BQU models emerged and the audience crooned at the pretty satiny slip.

The next ensemble got a lot of oohs and ahhs as models came out in the large flower-inspired T-shirt and tight boxer briefs.

Bridget continued with the presentation until they got to the two dresses she'd designed using the big flowers she was so fond of.

A roar went up from the audience and they all started clapping as the BQU strutted their stuff in the dresses. More vigorous clapping as the models showed off, with flair, a blouse made with the same big flowers worn with jeans, trousers and dress pants to show the well-designed blouse's versatility, and the fabric's strong selling points—comfort, beauty and ease of movement.

When the music stopped abruptly and the lights

came up, the flashes almost blinded her as her models lined up behind her showing a specially selected piece of lingerie or clothing.

The audience quieted down as a reporter raised her hand. "Tell us, Ms. Cole. Who is the wonderful inventor of this fabric and why is it so secret?"

Caught flat-footed, Bridget just stared at the woman. From the back a voice shouted, "Matt Fox, and he's right here."

All eyes turned toward the voice, Matt's ex-wife. A light focused on Matt. He looked like a deer caught in the headlights as flashbulbs went off in succession.

"Please, it's true that Dr. Fox invented the fabric, but what's really important is how it can be used in fashions," Bridget said, trying to get the focus off Matt and back onto her and the purpose of the fashion show.

"So you're nothing but a figurehead?" a reporter yelled out.

Her stomach knotted. "I've been the one to market..."

"But you've been fronting for the true inventor of the fabric? Isn't that right?"

"Yes, that's right." More flashbulbs went off and Bridget backed away from the podium.

Clarice pushed to Bridget's side followed by two other women. Clarice blurted, "I want to place orders."

"For the fabric?" Bridget asked.

"No, for your designs."

One of the other women held out a card. "Hi, I'm Serena Carr from Richler's in Boston and I want to talk about stocking your creations."

"Me, too. Nancy Carmichael from Louis and Winston."

Bridget backed away. She felt a hand on her arm and she turned to find Sheila Bowden.

"Come with me," she said, as reporters started pushing into the back, firing questions at her in such a jumble that Bridget couldn't understand what they were saying.

She followed Sheila up into her studio where Danny was gathering the last of the models' clothing and shooing them out the door. "What a coup," he whispered to her. "I could hear the noise from up here. I'd say you were a hit, honey."

"Could you give us a moment, Danny," Sheila said.

"Sure. No problem. I'll see you at the celebration party, kiddo. Don't be late."

Bridget had almost forgotten they were going to meet at The Salt Box after the show to celebrate. Her head pounded as Sheila steered her toward the chaise where Matt had made love to her. She sank down onto the cushion. Sheila was busy in the small kitchenette while dread circled through Bridget. Matt had been exposed, his secret revealed to everyone. She had no doubt that the story of Almost Naked, Inc. would be on the front page of the style section in all the Boston papers tomorrow.

She thought about how much he hated to have his privacy breached and now… "Oh God," she groaned.

Now, it was public. So very, very public and all because of her.

"Here, drink this. I saw you go white out there. What's wrong?"

"Matt," she said softly taking a sip of tea. "I've failed him."

BRIDGET WENT to the party and made a good showing, hiding all that she was feeling inside as easily as keeping a lid on that box. These people, who had given so generously of their time, deserved her attention and praise. They had helped make the show a smashing success.

Naomi was inundated with orders for the fabric that would just about clear out the stock they had on hand. She'd stayed behind to call the manufacturer to start production on the orders they couldn't fill from stock.

And, the department stores were clamoring for her designs, wanting to know what she had on hand which, of course, was virtually nothing. She had to put them off because she couldn't deal with that part of the fallout of the fashion show.

Morning dawned after an interminable night of tossing and turning. Bridget felt miserable down to her toes. This contract should have made her the happiest person on the planet, but leaving Matt felt like torture.

Naomi met her in her aunt's kitchen and asked, "Are you doing okay?"

"Yes. As well as can be expected."

"Have you spoken to Matt?"

"No, not yet. I'm getting my courage up. I promised him he wouldn't be exposed and he was. It must have been awful for him. Truth of the matter is I'm not so sure he wants to see me right now. He may never want to see me again."

"I can't believe that. You've made his business a success. So he got a little publicity. It'll die down. You know how the press is. They'll soon be after someone else. You've gotten everything you set out to get. You should enjoy yourself. Matt will come around."

Bridget couldn't agree.

Her aunt came into the kitchen and looked at her watch. "Bridget, we've got to get you to the airport. You must be so excited to be going back to New York."

"I am, Aunt Ida. You've been fabulous."

Her aunt smiled and they hugged. Bridget's throat closed up. She'd been able to confide in Matt and Naomi about what kind of shape her life had been in, but she'd never really come clean with her aunt.

"Aunt Ida, I have something I need to tell you."

"Sure. Come sit on the porch."

When they were settled in the swing, Bridget took her aunt's hands. "You've always been there for me, even now. I was broke when I came here. I had nothing left."

"Why didn't you tell me, I would have…"

"I know. I was ashamed to tell you or Mom about my problems. I didn't want you to see me in a bad light. I've done it all my life, kept everything that wasn't perfect from you and Mom. But now, after going through all this and realizing how important friends are in my life, I absolutely realize how vitally important family is. I love you, Aunt Ida, so much and I'll never varnish the truth ever again."

"I love you, too, Bridget. Nothing will ever change that."

They hugged again and Bridget said, "I'd better go say goodbye to Matt before I go."

It took all the strength she could muster to knock on his door. When he opened it, he didn't say anything, just backed up and let her in.

She went past him and climbed the stairs and she heard Matt come swiftly up behind her.

"What do you think you're doing?"

She continued into his room and into his bathroom. She picked up the toothbrush he'd bought for her. He was right behind her. "I want my toothbrush."

She gazed at his reflection in the mirror and he looked so forlorn, she had to drop her eyes. She left the bathroom and walked to the telescope.

"After getting a taste of what it's like in the limelight, I'm more resolved than ever. I can't live in a fishbowl," he said, coming up alongside her and looking out the window.

"I know, but I *have* to go." Bridget bent down and looked through the telescope. "You like this world you live in. I understand that. But there's a world out there, Matt. You look at the stars every night and wish. I want to reach for the stars and hold them in my hands. If you don't embrace life, you can't experience life. It's nothing but an observation just like looking through a piece of glass."

He didn't look at her, but kept staring out the window. "When are you leaving?"

"Now." It was an impossible dream to think that they could carry on a relationship long-distance.

"Matt, I'm so glad I came back and got to know you again. I don't know what to say, except you have been the best friend I've ever had. I'm sorry I let you down. I really hope it doesn't affect you at work. I know how much you wanted that tenured job."

When he didn't respond, Bridget wiped at the tears slipping down her cheeks. "Listen. Your business is in great hands. Naomi will make a great CEO. Thanks for being there when I needed you."

He nodded. "Naomi will work out fine. Take care of yourself. Goodbye, Bridget."

MATT STOOD AND LOOKED OUT the window for a long time after Bridget left. She had held nothing back, and what she had given him had been real—her passion, her need. She loved him, but her need to succeed was more powerful. He clenched his jaw against the hard pressure in his chest. He closed his eyes, realizing that he'd let the best thing in his life slip out the door. But how could he have stopped her? She was hell-bent on success and she couldn't see that it was nothing compared to what they had shared. He loved her and he had to let her go. That kind of life was not for him.

He turned to look at the brown-paper-wrapped

picture that had been delivered today. He'd bought the nude of Bridget from Sheila Bowden as soon as it was complete. All he would have of her was her likeness hanging on his wall.

14

BRIDGET SAT STILL, staring in the dressing table mirror while her makeup artist brushed blush on her cheeks. The woman in the mirror stared back, looking so glamorous in a chic plum halter evening dress sparkling with sequins and Swarovski crystals, Bridget almost didn't recognize herself.

That was the trouble these days. After Maggie unveiled her Independent Woman campaign, Bridget had become an overnight success and her life had been a whirlwind of activity and adventure for the last eight months. Bridget had everything she had ever dreamed possible—money, fame, respect in the business. Except there was something missing, something vital.

"All done, sweetums," Kevin, her makeup artist, said with one last flourish of the brush. The backs of her eyes stung. He reminded her so much of Danny.

"Thanks," she said, slipping out of the chair to make room for another model.

Tonight, during Fashion Week, on one of the coldest nights in February, she was fulfilling her last contractual obligation for Maggie Winterbourne, an informal fashion show staged in an art gallery. Maggie had shamelessly stolen Bridget's idea.

Bridget had been inundated with orders for her designs, but hadn't shown anything new since. Unable to deal with the fallout of her short time as a CEO and marketing whiz of a start-up company, she'd relegated her designing talent to the back burner.

She closed her eyes, waiting for her cue as she stood at the entrance to the room where she would hit key points on the floor while people enjoyed their tea and petits fours.

Talent. That word still made her stop and think. All her life she'd thought her sewing and designing had been nothing but doodling, not worth mentioning and certainly not worth pursuing. Her mother's expectations had overwhelmed her and at age six she didn't stand a chance.

But she wasn't six anymore.

Now she couldn't stop the creative energy that surged in her every day. She had dozens and dozens of drawings filling up one whole sketch pad, numerous patterns littering her bedroom desk and fabric always running through her brand-new sewing machine.

Maggie began speaking. As soon as she cued her, Bridget stepped out from behind the curtained alcove and hit her first pose. The applause beat against her ears and the lights blinded her. She walked forward to the next point like a wooden puppet and then the next, where she was supposed to stay for five minutes then make it back for her second outfit.

Her position afforded her an unobstructed view of the wall to her right. She recognized Sheila Bowden's work the moment she saw it. She studied the six pieces of art. They were all studies of a nude man. The curve of his jaw and the line of his back, the way he held himself looked achingly familiar. She broke her pose, stepping closer. Some of the guests sitting at the table closest to her glanced at her. Could it be? Could it possibly be Matt?

Her heart leaped in her chest. It was him. She could tell by that unmistakable spiky hair and the full clean lines of a body she knew by memory. Realizing her unprofessional breach, she pulled her eyes from him and made her way back to the dressing area. Her heart just a little bit lighter.

Once the show was over, she received many invitations to go to a popular nightclub, but Bridget shook her head and declined. She went back to Sheila's nude. She stood there so long the owner came over and touched her on the shoulder. "Beautiful, isn't he?"

"Yes, he is. I'll take the one of him in profile with his back to the artist."

"I'll wrap it up for you."

Bridget carried the piece home to her loft. All she had now was regrets. Regret that she had hurt Matt so much. Memories flooded her so strongly she had to close her eyes. Matt's hands, his mouth, the whispered words as he'd taken her on Sheila's chaise. The way he looked the last time she'd seen him.

Bridget clenched her jaw against an almost suffocating surge of love.

Hanging on to her emotions by a thread, she turned on the shower, stripped out of her clothes, the designer labels suddenly chafing her. With soap, she vigorously washed the makeup off her face. She leaned hard against the shower's tiles and closed her eyes. Her throat tightened and she swallowed against the awful feeling of vertigo that washed over her. She shivered in the hot water pouring from the spout, cupping her hands on her upper arms, trying to provide some self-warmth.

She opened her eyes and the box inside her burst open and all her emotions scattered like leaves caught by a powerful wind. They twisted inside her, opening up a vortex until she was overcome by them. Slowly she slid down the tiles until she was sitting in the tub, shaking.

Now was the time for her to be true to herself. Now was the time to admit when she was wrong. She'd made a horrible mistake that could have cost her everything. *Everything.*

Matt was everything.

Maggie's contract couldn't buy her happiness. A million contracts couldn't buy her happiness or self-worth because that had to come from inside. She'd been crippled all these years by the need to be what her mother so desperately wanted for her. But as Bridget sat there with the water rushing over her head, she felt a deep well of emptiness open. Who was she? What did she want out of life?

She closed her eyes and her voice caught on a sob. Matt. It had to have taken a boatload of courage on his part to pose nude. If he had the courage to change his life like that, she couldn't do any less and be worthy of his love. She wanted Matt. She wanted to go to bed with him every night; she wanted to wake up to him every morning. She wanted to laugh with him, tease him and make love to him.

Her fear of failing her mother's dream had blinded her to what was important in her life. Love, fulfillment and need.

She needed. She needed Matt. She needed her family and friends.

She could hardly remember a time in her life that she didn't feel the need to be "the best." To be the most beautiful, have the best clothes, live in the grandest home. Well, no more. Searching her heart and soul, throwing away that image other people had of her, Bridget rose in the tub like a phoenix from the ashes—a new woman.

"WHAT DID YOU JUST SAY?"

"I want out, Leslie."

Leslie's eyes widened, her brows raised. "What do you mean?"

"I mean I don't want to do this anymore. I'm leaving New York and going back to Cambridge."

"For a visit?"

"No. Forever."

"You're quitting?"

"Yes."

"I just moved your composite to the high board today. Now that your contract with Maggie has expired, she wants you to sign again with her. She's not the only designer who's clamoring for you. I've gotten interest from people in Hollywood—movie scripts. You can't be serious."

"I'm very serious. I've already put my loft up for sale. Thank you for everything, Leslie, but I'm going home."

"YOU'RE GOING HOME?"

"Yes. Naomi, I'll explain everything to you when I get to Cambridge. Could you call an emergency meeting of the BQU for me for tomorrow morning? Thanks. Ask them to meet at my mother's house."

Bridget hung up the phone and packed her suitcase and grabbed the nude of Matt and left the room without looking back.

The flight was short and she was soon hugging Aunt Ida.

"Could you drive me to my mother's house?"

"Of course."

When Bridget showed up at her mother's house, her mother was shocked, but delighted to see her. "Come in, dear."

Once they walked into the living room, Bridget

said to her aunt and her mother, "You might want to sit down."

"Why?" her mother asked.

"I quit."

"What?" they both said in unison.

"I want to be a designer."

Her mother rose and walked up to her. For a long moment she stared into Bridget's eyes, then she wrapped her arms around her and hugged her close. "Good for you. I'm so very proud of you."

She wasn't sure what she expected her mother to do, but this wasn't it.

Shortly after her mother's astonishing turnaround, the BQU started to arrive. She hugged all the Queens and sat down on her mother's designer sofa.

"I have a proposition for you all. I've decided to become a designer." There was a cheer from the group. "I want to give you all the opportunity to get in on the ground floor. Bottom line is—I need help."

"I'm in," Danny said. "I think you'll be as big as Maggie Winterbourne."

"Bigger," said Betty Sue. "I'm in."

All the other Queens made it unanimous.

"What are you going to use as your label?" Danny asked.

Bridget smiled and laughed before saying, "BQU. What else?"

Bridget rose from the sofa. "Now it's time to find a place to rent or buy depending on the property."

"Wait one second," her mother said from the door-way. "I want in."

"You do?" Bridget said, staring at her mother.

"Yes, I do and I have the perfect property."

"Who owns it?"

"I do."

"Isn't that convenient," Danny said, throwing his arm around her mother's shoulders.

Her mother looked up at him. "Do I know you?"

"You sure do," he said, "But you know me as Danielle."

"Oh my," Bridget's mother said.

BRIDGET STOOD in the storefront two doors down from the Bowden Gallery and sanded her office wall in preparation for the vibrant yellow paint she'd bought at the local hardware store. Her mother, dressed in jeans and a ratty shirt, sanded one of the other walls.

"You know I have a beautiful Queen Anne's desk in the attic. It belonged to your grandmother. I think it would look very elegant in here."

"I think you're right. Mom, why didn't you pro-test when I told you that I wanted to be a designer?"

"I haven't been able to forget the day of my gar-den party. I was so intent on showing you around to my friends, having you regale them with stories of Paris and New York. I didn't once think about you at all. And then Matt shouted at me that he loved you. I realized then that I've been so selfish and narrow-minded. When you came home instead of staying at your aunt Ida's, I was overjoyed. I so wanted my daughter back, but I didn't know how to go about it."

Bridget laughed. "I think you figured it out okay."

Her mother's eyes shone with emotion. She nodded. "This will make you happy?"

"Yes, I had a wake-up call. I don't want to measure my success that way anymore. I've been designing clothes since I was a little girl. Doodling, you used to call it. It never occurred to me until I met Matt that I could do it for a living."

Her mother stopped sanding and turned to look at her over her shoulder. "All the publicity from that job with Matt made you think this would be right for you?"

"No, the publicity was just a by-product. It was the great personal satisfaction I got from creating. It was like a high and I realize that trying is what's important. My personal self-worth is not tied to it. If I succeed or don't succeed, you'll still love me, Aunt Ida will still love me and my friends will still be there for me."

"I will be there for you, Bridget. I promise. I'm sure Matt is a fine young man. I was influenced by how your stepfather viewed my aspirations when we were first married. If I had pursued a career instead of getting pregnant, I'm not sure how happy I would be right now."

"Sounds like you and dad worked on your differences."

"We have. I think he understands a lot more now how I feel and he loves me. That's all that really matters."

"That's wonderful, Mom." Bridget sanded a bad patch on the wall, feeling as if layers were being peeled from her in strips. "There's something else I need to tell you. Before, when I came back to Cambridge because I not only lost my contract with Kathleen Armstrong, but I couldn't get any other work, I was also flat broke." It felt so good to finally tell her mother the truth.

"Thank you for confiding in me, Bridget. Now, we'd better get a move on. I think it's time to paint."

Fresh new beginnings.

It took a week to get her designer office and workspace completed. All the Queens were present when Bridget hung up her sign. In bold pink letters, it read BQU.

All the Queens decided that their days of garden parties and the life of leisure weren't as exciting as putting time and effort into an investment. Danny became her head seamstress and Betty Sue was a natural at choosing fabrics. Even her mother participated by organizing everyone so that her office ran like clockwork. Everything was in place in her life, except one thing.

Matt.

She was going after him with everything she had.

He was the only man for her.

MATT HELD THE FLOWERS so tight in his hand he thought he'd break the stems. When Bridget's mother opened the door, he expected to see the disapproval in her eyes. He even expected her to shut the door right in his face.

But she smiled brightly and said, "Matt. How wonderful to see you. Are you here for Bridget? Silly me, of course you are. She's in the greenhouse watering the plants. When you're through, perhaps you'd like to join her father and me for some lunch in the garden.

"Let me take your coat." She hung it up and then took his arm.

He was utterly speechless as he stared down at her blond head. Slamming into the side of the library door with his shoulder didn't even faze her.

"Do be careful not to hurt yourself."

At the entrance to the greenhouse, she let go of his arm. "We'll see you later."

Matt stood there and took a deep breath. Walking forward, he could hear Bridget humming that tune she'd been singing in the shower. When he turned the corner, avoiding a large table of orchids, he saw her.

His throat closed up. "Bridget."

She started and dropped the hose. It snaked around like a wild beast. She chased it and Matt helped her, drenching them both before he finally got smart and turned it off at its source.

Breathless, her hair dripping water into her eyes, she stared up at him and his now worse-for-wear flowers.

"What are these? They're beautiful."

"*Trientalis borealis*. Starflower. Now you can hold them in your hands."

Her eyes welled up with tears and in the past that would have been enough to make him close up his emotions for fear she would cross his boundaries, but now he accepted her just the way she was.

"I'm a fool," he said softly. "A rigid fool. You are right. I did stand back from life instead of embrace it. But I've changed."

"I saw the portrait, Matt."

He colored, obviously still not as comfortable as he wanted to be. "Did you like it?"

"I saw the whole series she did on you, but I bought the one where you're in profile with your back to the artist. You have a really nice butt."

He colored again and laughed. "It was the hardest thing I've ever done." Unable to wait one second longer he took her into his arms. His throat closed up again, and he buried his nose in her wet hair, a surge of hard emotion cutting through him. A sense of relief filtered through him as her arms came up around his neck to hold him close.

"I can't go back and fix the past, Bridget, but the present is all new and clean. I can get a job in New York. I can live with your lifestyle. Anything you want."

"Come with me," she said, taking his hand.

"I'll follow you to the moon, sweetheart."

Those words were like manna from heaven and Bridget soaked them up like a sponge. Keeping a firm grip on his wrist, half afraid he would vanish like smoke before her eyes. Dripping wet, she walked through the house to a sumptuous bedroom done in gold tones. She picked up a vase on her bedside, the glass cool to the touch. Heading for the balcony, she threw the flowers over the side. In the adjoining bathroom, she filled the vase and set the delicate white five-point flowers inside. Her throat tight, she replaced the vase on her night table.

He reached for her, but she evaded his grasp. "Wait a second. There's something I need to say to you. Sit on the bed."

He complied while she made her way to the French doors and leaned against the jamb, the wood a hard goad to keep her focused on what she had to say. "I made some bad choices when it came to you, Matt, and I need to tell you I'm sorry about that."

"Bridget, we both made mistakes."

"But you were trying to change. I know how hard it was to let me invade your privacy. I know you struggled with it, but you loved me and you tried to overcome it. I, on the other hand, didn't make an effort to see what kind of path I was walking."

"I'm listening."

"I always thought of myself as the little engine that could. Everything I have ever committed time and energy to doing, I've done from a competitive, striving, goal-oriented stance. Performing everything as close to perfect as possible has fueled my existence since I was six. The reason—fear—the fear of failing. To fail meant death, swallowed up by a black hole. I had to avoid it at all costs."

"Go on," he urged.

"I was repeatedly rewarded for my beauty and I became practiced at adjusting myself so much that I lost touch with myself. Having a successful image feeds on itself and obliterated my own core identity. The more successful the image, the more tempting it was for me to continue to rely on it and to develop it rather than myself. Who I really am became more and more unknown territory, something I didn't want to focus on because if I looked inward, I'd feel empty.

"I didn't really know who I was beyond that image, so it was everything to me to maintain it. That's why I went back to New York to sign that contract."

"Then you saw the nude?"

"Yes. As I said, your courage humbled me and when you gave me the opportunity to be the CEO of your business, you gave me the chance to see myself in another light. I could do something beyond projecting this image to the world. I found friends and got so much value from the experience. I want to be a designer, Matt, and stay here in Cambridge. My only regret is failing you in the end."

"You didn't fail me. I realized that I had been protecting myself, not my reputation at MIT. My chairperson was overjoyed with the publicity. I've gotten the tenure track position, but that's not important to me anymore."

"Then we're even, because I've got the two things I most want in life."

"What are those?"

"A job I know I can really do and, success or failure, it will be mine."

"And the other thing?"

"It's not a thing, Matt. It's a person. A wonderful, understanding, beautiful person. You." Walking up to him, she snagged the tab of his jeans and opened it, pulling down the zipper. "Now let me see that nice ass."

"I'll show you mine if you show me yours," he said with a grin and that adorable flush colored his face again. She loved that he was still just a little bit self-conscious of his nudity. It made him so endearing and human.

He cupped her face and, feeling as if she was drowning, drugged by sensation, paralyzed by his touch, she waited. He tipped her face up and slowly lowered his head. Bridget made a helpless sound and let her eyes drift shut. Exerting pressure on her jaw, he opened her mouth, then covered it in a wet, deep, searching kiss that drove every ounce of strength out of her body and made her knees buckle.

Gathering her up in a hard, enveloping embrace, he drew her between his thighs, working his mouth hungrily against hers, drawing her hips even closer until she was straddling him. Bridget couldn't breathe, she couldn't think; all she could do was hang on and ride out the thousand sensations exploding in her. Matt caught her hips and molded her flush against him, his mouth wide and hot as he ran his hand under her damp tank top and up her back. He emitted a low sound of approval when he encountered nothing but bare skin, and he slid his hand up her bare torso, cupping her breast, stroking her with his thumb.

His touch drove the breath right out of her, and she made another helpless sound against his mouth. Matt tightened his arm around her back and dragged his mouth away, his breathing labored. Her heart racing and her pulse thick and heavy, she turned her face against his neck, the warmth of his hand filling her with a heavy weakness.

He slid both hands up her rib cage and under her top. Drawing a deep, unsteady breath, he eased away from her and spoke, his voice very gruff. "Lift your arms."

Bridget eagerly complied, her breath jamming in her chest as he stripped the garment from her. His breathing ragged, he yanked his shirt free of his jeans, and Bridget weakly rested her head against his jaw, her whole body starting to unravel.

When he rubbed his chest against her naked breasts, she called his name roughly and he covered her mouth again. She drank in the moistness of his mouth, drawing his tongue deeper and deeper, and he rolled her nipples again as a frenzy of need seized her. Inhaling raggedly, he twisted on the bed to dump her off his lap. He stood and stripped off his jeans.

He undid her jeans and slid his hands under her panties. His hands splayed wide on her hips, he slowly, slowly shoved everything down, his mouth grazing her collarbone, the tip of one breast, her midriff.

He climbed onto the bed. Drawing air through clenched teeth, he pushed her thighs open. Bridget's senses went into overload when his body connected with hers, the feel of him thick and hard and fully aroused at the juncture of her thighs driving the breath from her. Grasping the back of her head, he covered her mouth with another blistering kiss, his fingers tangling in her hair, his heart hammering against her. Tightening his hold on her head, he wedged his knee between her legs then pressed her onto her back, and Bridget fought for breath as he settled heavily between her thighs. The feel of him was almost too much.

Feeling as if she was drowning in the thick, pulsating sensations, Bridget shuddered and turned her face against him as he worked his way down her neck, his touch turning her boneless. Sinking into sensation, sinking into unbelievable pleasure.

He took his time, savoring her neck, the hollow behind her ear, the sensitive part under her jaw, and then he returned to her mouth, kissing her with a thoroughness that went on and on. Dragging his mouth away, he shuddered and turned his head against hers, the muscles in his back bunching as he flexed his hips against her one more time.

It was too much. Bridget cried out his name and arched against him, her body tightening, tightening as she clutched at his back and lifted her hips. Matt pushed his arm under her hips and shifted, then, with an agonized groan, he thrust into her, burying himself in her swollen, wet heat. His whole body went rigid, and he roughly adjusted his hold. Gathering strength, he thrust into her again and again. Bridget came apart in his arms, the tightness converging into one throbbing center exploded, and convulsions ripped through her, making her arch and cry out. Clutching her head against him, Matt locked his arm around her hips, thrusting again and again; then he made a ragged sound and shuddered violently in her arms, his release as cataclysmic as hers.

Bridget hung on to him and turned her face against his neck, the emotional aftermath as wrenching as the release—she felt raw and was weeping and in a million pieces. As if it took the last bit of energy he had, Matt adjusted his hold, his hand splayed wide at the back of her head, holding her with such absolute tenderness that it made her throat close up all over again. He could turn her inside out, and how she loved him.

He held her for a long time, until his breathing leveled out and she stopped shaking, until the aftermath softened into something less intense.

Bracing his weight on his forearms, he cupped her face, wiping away the traces of tears with his thumbs. Then with a heavy sigh, he lowered his head and gave her the sweetest, softest kiss. Releasing another sigh, he lifted his head and gazed down at her, a glint of intimate amusement in his eyes. "I can't believe we just did it in your mother's house. The greenhouse was one thing, but this... She invited me to lunch, you know."

Her throat still unbearably tight, she looked at him, trying to blink away the tears. Swallowing against the clog of emotion, she smoothed her hand up his long, muscled back. "Did she? Looks like my mother changed, too. And all because of what you said."

"Me? What did I say?"

"At the garden party. You asked her if she realized how selfish she was."

He smiled sheepishly. "I was agitated and I wanted to tell you I loved you. She was pulling you away to go talk about frivolous things and I had this love burning in my gut."

He shifted his hips, and Bridget gripped him as her expression altered. "Don't go," she whispered, her voice suddenly uneven.

His expression turning serious, he lowered his head and brushed a light kiss against her mouth. "I'm not moving," he whispered huskily. "I'll stay here as long as you want me to."

"Forever," she murmured.

"Forever?" he said chuckling, and moved inside her, as he moistened her bottom lip. "I can give it my best shot."

She sighed and moved beneath him, caught in the way he made her feel as if she was sinking into something sweet, warm and utterly safe.

"But, I might need a trip to New York City every

once in a while and I really need to plan a trip to Italy. I heard it's wonderful."

She hit his shoulder. "Think you're pretty cute, huh?"

"More like devastatingly cute," he said, bending down and fumbling around on the floor. When he came back up, he held a black velvet box in his hand.

"Oh, Matt." She took the box and opened the lid, her breath jammed in her throat. Tears spilled out of her eyes as she removed the ring from the box and slipped it on her finger. "We'll balance each other out beautifully. You'll see."

"I have no doubt. I love you so much, Bridget."

She looked up into his soft amber eyes and said with finality and love, "Me, too. Forever."

HARLEQUIN® *Blaze*™

Women can upgrade their airline seats,
wardrobes and jobs. If only we could
upgrade our men....

The Man-Handlers
Women who know how to get the best from their men

Join author Karen Kendall as she shows us
how three smart women make over their men
until they get newer, sexier versions!

Catch these irresistible men in

#195 WHO'S ON TOP?
August 2005

#201 UNZIPPED?
September 2005

#207 OPEN INVITATION?
October 2005

Don't miss these fun, sexy stories from Karen Kendall!
Look for these books at your favorite retail outlet.

www.eHarlequin.com   HBTMH0805

Silhouette®
Desire.

Available this August from
Silhouette Desire and *USA TODAY*
bestselling author

Jennifer Greene

HOT TO THE TOUCH
(Silhouette Desire #1670)

Locked in the darkness of his tortured soul and
body, Fox Lockwood has tried to retreat from
the world. Hired to help, massage therapist
Phoebe Schneider relies on her sense of touch
to bring Fox back. But will they be able to keep
their relationship strictly professional once their
connection turns unbelievably hot?

Available wherever Silhouette Books are sold.

Visit Silhouette Books at www.eHarlequin.com   SDHTTT0705

If you enjoyed what you just read,
then we've got an offer you can't resist!

Take 2 bestselling
love stories FREE!
Plus get a FREE surprise gift!

Clip this page and mail it to Harlequin Reader Service®

IN U.S.A.
3010 Walden Ave.
P.O. Box 1867
Buffalo, N.Y. 14240-1867

IN CANADA
P.O. Box 609
Fort Erie, Ontario
L2A 5X3

YES! Please send me 2 free Harlequin® Blaze™ novels and my free surprise gift. After receiving them, if I don't wish to receive anymore, I can return the shipping statement marked cancel. If I don't cancel, I will receive 6 brand-new novels each month, before they're available in stores! In the U.S.A., bill me at the bargain price of $3.99 plus 25¢ shipping and handling per book and applicable sales tax, if any*. In Canada, bill me at the bargain price of $4.47 plus 25¢ shipping and handling per book and applicable taxes**. That's the complete price and a savings of at least 10% off the cover prices—what a great deal! I understand that accepting the 2 free books and gift places me under no obligation ever to buy any books. I can always return a shipment and cancel at any time. Even if I never buy another book from Harlequin, the 2 free books and gift are mine to keep forever.

151 HDN D7ZZ
351 HDN D72D

Name	(PLEASE PRINT)
Address	Apt.#
City	State/Prov. Zip/Postal Code

Not valid to current Harlequin® Blaze™ subscribers.

Want to try two free books from another series?
Call 1-800-873-8635 or visit www.morefreebooks.com.

* Terms and prices subject to change without notice. Sales tax applicable in N.Y.
** Canadian residents will be charged applicable provincial taxes and GST.
   All orders subject to approval. Offer limited to one per household.
   ® and ™ are registered trademarks owned and used by the trademark owner and/or its licensee.

BLZ05   ©2005 Harlequin Enterprises Limited.

eHARLEQUIN.com

The Ultimate Destination for Women's Fiction

For **FREE online reading,** visit www.eHarlequin.com now and enjoy:

Online Reads
Read **Daily** and **Weekly** chapters from our Internet-exclusive stories by your favorite authors.

Interactive Novels
Cast your vote to help decide how these stories unfold...then stay tuned!

Quick Reads
For shorter romantic reads, try our collection of Poems, Toasts, & More!

Online Read Library
Miss one of our online reads? Come here to catch up!

Reading Groups
Discuss, share and rave with other community members!

For great reading online, visit www.eHarlequin.com today!

INTONL04R

HARLEQUIN® Blaze™

THRILLS, CHILLS...
AND SEX!

When $4.5 million of their grandfather's stamps
are stolen by a ruthless criminal, sisters Gwen and
Joss Chastain stop at nothing to get them back.

Catch their stories in SEALED WITH A KISS,
a brand-new miniseries from KRISTIN HARDY

#187 CERTIFIED MALE
June 2005

#199 U.S. MALE
August 2005

On sale at your favorite retail outlet.

Be sure to visit www.tryblaze.com
for more great Blaze books!

www.eHarlequin.com   HBUSMALE0805

HARLEQUIN® *Blaze*™

**Three sisters whose power between
the sheets can make men feel better
than they ever have…literally!**

Sexual Healing
Her magic touch makes those sheets sizzle

Join bestselling author Dorie Graham as
she tells the tales of women with ability
to heal through sex in

#196 THE MORNING AFTER
August 2005

#202 SO MANY MEN…
September 2005

#208 FAKING IT
October 2005

Be sure to catch this sensual miniseries
from Dorie Graham!

Look for these books at your favorite retail outlet.

www.eHarlequin.com   HBSH0805

HARLEQUIN®

Blaze™

COMING NEXT MONTH

#195 WHO'S ON TOP? Karen Kendall
The Man-Handlers, Bk. 1

In this battle between the sexes, they're both determined to win. Jane O'Toole is supposed to be assessing Dominic Sayers's work-related issues, but the sexual offers he delivers make it hard to stay focused. But once they hit the sheets, the real challenge is to see who's the most satisfied...

#196 THE MORNING AFTER Dorie Graham
Sexual Healing, Bk. 1

Not only did he stay until morning, he came back! Nikki McClellan can heal men through sex. And her so-called gift is powerful enough that a single time is all they need. At this rate she's destined to be a one-night wonder...until Dylan Cain. Which is a good thing, because he's so hot, she doesn't want to let him go!

#197 KISS & MAKEUP Alison Kent
Do Not Disturb, Bk. 3

Bartender Shandi Fossey is mixing cool cocktails temporarily at Hush—the hottest hotel in Manhattan. So what's a girl to do when sexy Quentin Marks offers to buy *her* a drink? The famous music producer can open a lot of doors for her—but all she really wants is to enter the door leading to his suite....

#198 TEXAS FIRE Kimberly Raye

Sociology professor Charlene Singer has always believed that it's what's on the outside that counts. That's got her...nowhere. So she's going to change her image and see if she gets any luckier. Only, she soon realizes she'll need more than luck to handle rodeo cowboy Mason McGraw....

#199 U.S. MALE Kristin Hardy
Sealed with a Kiss, Bk. 2

Joss Chastain has a taste for revenge. Her family's stamps worth $4.5 million have been stolen, and Joss will stop at nothing to get them back, even if it means seducing private eye John "Bax" Baxter into helping her. As tensions rise and the chemistry ignites, Joss and Bax must risk everything to outsmart the criminal mastermind...and stay alive.

#200 WHY NOT TONIGHT? Jacquie D'Alessandro
24 Hours: Blackout, Bk. 2

When Adam Clayton fills in at his friend's photography studio, he never dreamed he'd be taking *boudoir* photos—of his old flame! Too bad Mallory *has* a boyfriend—or, at least she *did* before she caught him cheating. She's not heartbroken, but she is angry. Lucky for Adam, a blackout gives him a chance to make her forget anyone but him...

www.eHarlequin.com

HBCNM0705